Will Irma Taranee Cornelia Hay Lin

Whispers of Doubt

Adapted by ALICE ALFONSI

HarperCollins *Children's Books*

This book was first published in the USA in 2004 by Volo/Hyperion Books for Children
First published in Great Britain in 2007 by HarperCollins *Children's Books*, a division of
HarperCollins Publishers Ltd.

© 2007 Disney Enterprises, Inc.

ISBN13: 978-0-00-722222-3
ISBN10: 0-00-722222-X

1 3 5 7 9 10 8 6 4 2

The HarperCollins website is:
www.harpercollinschildrensbooks.co.uk

Visit www.clubwitch.co.uk

Printed and bound in Italy

MRS. RUDOLPH HAS TAUGHT AT OUR SCHOOL FOR A LONG TIME, BUT NOW SHE'S DECIDED TO ENJOY A WELL-DESERVED REST.

THE PARTY? REMEMBER?

N-O-O-O! I DON'T REMEMBER A THING.

IT'S HOPELESS.

AND AS SHE'LL BE GOING INTO RETIREMENT NEXT WEEK, SHE WANTED TO BRING YOU ALL TOGETHER HERE TO SAY GOODBYE.

STAY A LITTLE WHILE LONGER!

WE'LL REALLY MISS YOUR QUIZZES!

YEAH, NOBODY GAVE BETTER GRADES THAN YOU DID!

CLAP

CLAP CLAP

I JUST WANTED TO TELL YOU ALL THAT TEACHING AT THIS SCHOOL HAS BEEN A WONDERFUL ADVENTURE. I HOPE I MANAGED TO MAKE YOU ALL SEE WHAT MAGIC THERE IS IN NUMBERS.

I WANT ALL OF YOU TO KNOW THAT EVEN A SIMPLE NUMBER LIKE FIVE CAN HOLD A MARVELLOUS, UNKNOWN UNIVERSE WITHIN IT.

AND THAT I'LL MISS ALL OF YOU!

I DON'T KNOW ABOUT "MAR-VELLOUS"...

IT'S OUR TURN NOW! WHAT DO WE DO?

JUST SMILE. I'LL THINK OF SOMETHING!

AND NOW, LET'S HAVE A ROUND OF APPLAUSE FOR MR. HORSEBERG, WHO WILL BE REPLACING ME.

HORSE-WHAT? HORSEBERG? HORSE-FACE?

WHERE IS HE?

CLAP

CLAP

I'M RIGHT HERE, GIRLS. AND I HEARD THAT!

GULP...

AS PRINCIPAL OF SHEFFIELD INSTITUTE, I AM PROUD TO GIVE THE FLOOR TO MISS COOK.

THE PARTY FOR MRS. RUDOLPH TOMORROW...

COME ON, TARANEE! YOU CAN DO IT!

ONE

Some days a girl just has to take a break to save her sanity, Will told herself as she strolled along Heatherfield's wide sidewalks trying to clear her head.

School had been relentlessly long that day. Lessons had dragged on forever, and the teachers had all seemed to be speaking in slow motion. By seventh period – no surprise – Will had actually dozed off. Thank goodness Cornelia had nudged her awake before her head hit the desk. That was when she'd asked Will to go shopping with her in downtown Heatherfield after school.

Will had never been a shopaholic. That was Cornelia's thing. But the way the stresses in her life had been piling up lately, buying a cool new hat sounded a lot more appealing than deciphering a mysterious diary, protecting the universe from evil, or guessing when Matt Olsen was going to ask her out again.

So far, Will had followed Cornelia into two department stores, three trendy boutiques, and one antique shop. The colourful store windows and crisp fall air were far more energising than the stuffy, heated classrooms of the Sheffield Institute. But Cornelia had yet to find the perfect class gift for their retiring maths teacher, Mrs. Rudolph. And Will had yet to find peace regarding the things that had happened over the past few weeks – not to mention the past few hours.

For one thing, Will still felt badly about snapping at Hay Lin. The Air Guardian had always tried to cheer everyone up with her good-natured optimism, especially Will. But the girl's obsession with that mysterious diary was driving Will crazy.

The leather-bound journal had been given to Will by Kadma, the elderly ex-Guardian who lived in Will's old hometown. Unfortunately, the diary had yet to be helpful – because it was totally unreadable. Every page had been written in some kind of weird code that involved planets, stars, and strange, indecipherable symbols.

Hay Lin had suggested they take the diary to her new friend Eric Lyndon at the Heatherfield Observatory. Eric was into stuff like that, so Hay Lin thought he might be able to make sense of the arrangement of planets and stars.

When Eric couldn't read it, he'd showed it to his grandfather, a brilliant, eccentric astronomer; Professor Zachary Lyndon now had the diary and was working on translating it.

The last thing Will wanted to do just then, however, was visit the old professor for a diary update. That was why she snapped so nastily at Hay Lin. The girl just didn't have a clue. She didn't know when to give it a rest.

"Why did you get so ticked off at Hay Lin?" Cornelia suddenly asked as they strolled in front of a framing and print shop. "After all, Eric and his grandfather are only trying to help us read the diary."

Will stopped. Great, she thought, now

Cornelia, too. It seems like everyone's obsessed with that stupid diary.

"You're right," she told Cornelia with a sigh. "I guess meeting Kadma just put me in a bad mood."

Cornelia looked confused, so Will tried to explain. "Ever since I found out I'd always been watched, everything seems to be getting on my nerves."

Will wasn't kidding about being watched. While she was growing up in Fadden Hills, Kadma and another ex-Guardian named Halinor had used a network of people to spy on Will. Some of her teachers, her beloved babysitter, a next-door neighbour, even her first swimming coach had been watching Will's every move.

"Look on the bright side," Cornelia replied. "Just try to think of it like this – a lot of people wanted to protect you."

"I've tried!" Will exclaimed. "But lately that's just been getting more and more difficult to do."

I don't think my friends realise how much that trip back to my hometown took out of me, thought Will. To me, Fadden Hills will never again be the pretty little town where I once lived. Now and forever, it will be the place where the people I knew and once trusted spied on me!

"And then they would report everything to Halinor," Kadma had confessed to Will during her visit. "You were her protégé."

That had been another shocker for Will. She had been the protégé of someone whom she had never even met! And never would, either. Halinor had passed away. And the only thing she'd left Will was a diary she couldn't even read.

Well, fine, thought Will. A part of her didn't really want to know what was in those weird pages anyway. In fact, it seemed that the more she learned about her role as Keeper of the Heart of Candracar, the more she had to worry about!

"Even the Heart of Candracar has changed," she finally confessed to Cornelia after a few moments of silence. It was hard for Will to talk about her fears concerning the Heart.

The Heart was a perfect, powerful crystal, which had been given to her by Yan Lin, Hay

Lin's late grandmother. Yan Lin had once been a Guardian herself, serving with Kadma and Halinor. She was the one who had first told the five friends about their powers: Irma controlled water; Taranee, fire; Cornelia, earth; and Hay Lin, air.

Will was the Keeper of the Heart. She held the Heart inside her body, and she could call up its magic at any time to magnify the powers of the other Guardians and unite them into one of the most awesome forces in the universe. It was the duty of the Guardians, as given to them by the great Oracle of Candracar, to use their powers to protect the earth – and other dimensions of the universe – from evil. And it was the duty of Will, as Keeper of the Heart, to lead the other Guardians in that quest.

The demands made on Will were overwhelming, especially for someone not used to being a leader. And she had struggled hard with them – at first, she would even become paralysed in the face of danger. But over time she had proven herself to be an inspiring, fearless, and capable leader of W.I.T.C.H. – the nickname the girls had given their group by combining the first letters of each of their names.

Lately, however, Will seemed to be facing an even bigger challenge than that posed by an evil enemy from without. The Heart itself, a heavy responsibility, was becoming harder and harder to carry within her.

"It weighs a ton, and it's red hot," Will whispered to Cornelia when she saw her friend looking at her expectantly. "It's like it's burning inside of me."

Even as she spoke, the Heart was growing heavier. Turning towards the shop window, she put a hand on the glass to steady herself, staring at a display of expensive frames and prints without really seeing them.

Cornelia was silent for a minute, as if thinking everything over. "Maybe that's what's causing you to be in such a bad mood these days," she gently suggested.

"Maybe," said Will. "All I know is that lately I've been feeling really exhausted and stressed and down."

Cornelia put an arm around Will's shoulders. "Well, promise me that you'll call whenever you feel that way."

A natural strength flowed from the earth Guardian. It seeped through Will's blue jacket, through her body, and into her spirit. It made her burden momentarily lighter. "Hey," Will said with a smile, "since when do you have such a soft heart?"

Will clearly remembered how brassy, opinionated, and stubborn Cornelia had once been – and, depending on the circumstances, could still be. But the truth was that Cornelia's experiences with Caleb had totally changed her.

Cornelia had fallen deeply in love with the handsome boy from Metamoor, then almost lost him. It had matured and mellowed her. She was more patient now, less selfish; braver and stronger, too.

Cornelia was also the only Guardian who knew, *really* knew, what Will was going through in her feelings for Matt and her struggles to make that relationship work. That shared knowledge had also helped to strengthen the bond between them. It was good to have somebody to talk with about boy troubles.

"See something you like?" asked a bright voice.

The startled girls looked up in surprise. A saleswoman had poked her head outside the door of the frame and print shop. The woman was elegant and blonde, dressed in a tailored lilac suit. A matching silk scarf was tied in a dainty bow around her neck, and pearls dangled from her ears.

"Um . . . I'm not sure, actually," said Will, awkwardly shifting in her battered trainers and brushing back her shaggy red mop of hair. She was too embarrassed to admit that she'd been staring at the woman's shop windows without actually *looking* at what was inside.

Cornelia, on the other hand, wasn't bothered in the least. The ultimate shopping pro, she gave the woman a confident smile. Beneath her powder-blue beret, Cornelia tossed her long, blonde hair over her shoulder and breezed inside. As her polished black boots carried her through the store, she quickly appraised the items on display.

There were photographs of city skylines and rolling country hills, and reproductions of Italian and French masterpieces. While Will examined some funky original modern-art posters, Cornelia walked over to take a closer look at a cluster of prints that featured Heatherfield landmarks.

Tapping her chin as she stood immersed in thought, Cornelia finally turned to the saleswoman. "Do you have a print of Sheffield Institute?"

Will raised her eyebrows in surprise. She would never have thought of a gift like that for a retiring maths teacher. But she had to admit, it really would be perfect!

"I have an old photograph in the back," the saleswoman told Cornelia. "Would you like to see it?"

"Certainly," Cornelia replied.

The saleswoman left the showroom for a minute. When she returned from the back room, she was carrying a large photograph in an antique gilded frame.

"It's beautiful!" Cornelia exclaimed. "I think it'd be the perfect retirement gift for Mrs. Rudolph."

"It dates back fifty years," said the saleswoman with a smile.

"What do you say, Will?" said Cornelia, beaming at the framed photograph. "Should we take it?"

As Will looked at the photograph, she heard the saleswoman's voice again. "She doesn't seem to care much about what you're going through, does she?"

Will's eyes widened, and she whipped around to face the saleswoman. "I beg your pardon?" she said. But the woman wasn't even looking at her.

Did I really hear her speak? Will wondered. Or was the voice only in my head? Am I losing my mind?

"Do you like it?" the saleswoman asked Cornelia.

"Will? What do you think?" Cornelia asked again. She held the photograph up for Will to have a better look.

"Looks fine to me," said Will, still rattled by what she had heard – or thought she had heard.

The saleswoman stepped closer. "You don't seem so convinced," she remarked.

Will gulped. Convinced of what? she wondered. Buying the framed photo or buying that comment about Cornelia?

The words played through Will's mind once more: *She doesn't seem to care much about what you're going through, does she?*

Up to that moment, Will had thought

Cornelia did care. But did she, really? There were many times in the past when Cornelia had acted in a self-absorbed and selfish manner . . . and now that Will thought about it, all Cornelia really did seem to care about at the moment was getting the class gift for Mrs. Rudolph. Why?

Because it will reflect back on her, of course, Will concluded. The more perfect the gift, the more perfect everyone at Sheffield will think she is. Especially because everyone contributed money for it –

Money! Where was the money?

"No, no, no!" Will suddenly exclaimed, searching through her pockets, then her backpack. "I can't remember where I put the envelope with the money we collected!"

I've lost it! Will wailed to herself. *I've lost it! My classmates will never talk to me again!*

"Will," said Cornelia firmly.

Will looked up. Cornelia was holding a white envelope thick with dollar bills.

"You gave it to me, remember?" Cornelia said.

Will knocked her head with her fist. "I'm a total scatterbrain today," she said with an embarrassed sigh.

Cornelia just smiled and smoothly asked the saleswoman, "Could you gift wrap that for us?"

Will closed her eyes and tried to get control of her raging anxiety. I'm really wrecked, she thought. It must be the stress of being the Keeper of the Heart. It's totally turning my brains to mush!

TWO

The Oracle of Candracar levitated within a dazzling column of pure, golden light. His small body, robed in white, knelt on nothing but air. His delicate hands were joined together in prayerful posture. And though his eyes were closed, he could see everything, not only within the crystal walls of the vast Temple, but beyond the clouds that surrounded them.

"Oracle?" Yan Lin called softly.

Without opening his eyes, the Oracle had sensed the woman's entrance into the meditation room. He was aware that she'd bowed her head and knelt behind him on the ornate floor, which was embedded with jewels from many worlds.

"I hear an edge of distress in your

voice, honourable Yan Lin," the Oracle told her in a calm tone.

"You know what it is," Yan Lin said. "A sad old story is repeating itself." The old woman's already wrinkled brow became even more creased with worry.

The Oracle felt his serenity seeping away as dark memories from the distant past descended upon him like unwanted storm clouds. He knew very well what Yan Lin was talking about. That "sad old story" had happened long ago, although it seemed much more recent. . . .

Back then, Yan Lin had been a young Guardian on earth. Kadma, Halinor, and Cassidy had been her fellow Guardians, along with Nerissa, who had served as Keeper of the Heart.

Nerissa had started out as a force for good, but over time she had changed completely. Coveting the Heart and its power for herself, she had forsaken her responsibilities as a Guardian and begun to use the Heart for selfish purposes.

Her fellow Guardian, Cassidy, had seen the danger. She'd warned the Oracle of the change in Nerissa. And the Oracle had responded by taking the Heart from Nerissa and giving it to Cassidy, making her its new Keeper.

Losing the Heart had enraged Nerissa. Half crazed with anger, jealousy, and greed, she'd murdered Cassidy in an evil and merciless act.

Cassidy's death had devastated her fellow Guardians. Together, Halinor, Kadma, and Yan Lin had apprehended Nerissa and brought her to Candracar for justice. The Oracle and the Congregation had tried Nerissa, found her guilty, and sentenced her to be entombed deep within a volcanic mountain for all eternity. Unfortunately, that hadn't been the end of the tragedy.

Kadma and Halinor had raged at the Oracle, blaming him for the death of Cassidy. The two were unable to understand or accept the horrible events that had happened. They could not find it within themselves to rise above it and move on as Yan Lin had. The Oracle had had no choice but to expel the two Guardians from Candracar.

The Oracle still mourned the loss of Cassidy, Halinor, Kadma, and even Nerissa, who had once been worthy and good, before her internal darkness had overwhelmed her.

Yan Lin is not wrong in her fears, he thought. The past could very well repeat itself.

But the Oracle knew that the choices of the new Guardians were their own to make. He could not change their independent minds. Nor could he lighten the weight of the Heart on its current Keeper.

In the end, Will would have to make her own choices, rise to the challenges before her. Events would have to play themselves out, even if it meant a repeat of the tragedy that had taken place so many years before.

"We cannot allow it!" Yan Lin cried, losing control of herself. "Won't you let me do something?"

The Oracle's calm vanished. His eyes opened wide. "That's enough, Yan Lin!" he firmly warned.

At times, even the Oracle was frustrated by his limitations, but he could not change the universal order.

"None of us can interfere in what others have decided!" he reminded her. "Therefore, I must ask you to keep your distance from the Guardians."

"As you wish," Yan Lin replied. She rose

from the ornate floor and quietly left the room.

I'll obey the rules, Yan Lin thought as she moved down the vast hallway. But that doesn't mean I can't talk to my sweet Hay Lin. After all, I'm still her grandmother!

The Oracle sighed. He had heard Yan Lin's thoughts. And he wasn't all that surprised by them. Before she had died and taken her place among the Elders of Candracar, Yan Lin had assembled the new generation of Guardians on earth. Of course, the closest connection she felt was to her own granddaughter.

The Oracle closed his eyes within the shimmering column of golden light. Focusing on the earth, he sought out the Guardian with power over air.

An image came to him. A pretty Asian girl with long blue-black pigtails walked through a city park. Around her, autumn leaves blazed red, orange, and brilliant yellow. A large building of white granite, with palladium windows and classical columns, rose before her. Its domed roof gleamed like polished ivory in the sun.

As the young Guardian approached the steps of the building, her almond-shaped eyes lit up. And her thoughts floated up to the Oracle like the gentle tinkling of wind chimes. . . .

Here's the observatory! I'm a bit early, but I'm dying of curiosity!

The Oracle watched the young Guardian climb the stone steps two at a time. She walked through the arched doorway of the Heatherfield Observatory. A boy was waiting.

"Eric!" she cried upon seeing her new friend. She took in the boy's large, intelligent brown eyes, tousled dark hair, and engaging smile.

"Hi, Hay Lin!" the boy said in greeting. He in turn gazed at her delicate features and petite form, clad in a short red skirt and bright green leg warmers.

A small smile came to the Oracle's lips. He could hear the flight of the young Guardian's heart, feel the racing blood in the handsome boy's veins. "Ah, young love," the Oracle murmured from his lofty perch. "Yet another instance of a force I can do little to change."

Even the first meeting of these two had been one of those rare instances of fate – an almost magical coincidence. The Oracle had observed it during one of his meditations.

On a warm day, Hay Lin had rolled unsteadily down to the ice-cream stand on her new in-line skates. She'd bought a cone and headed back down the road again. As Eric whizzed by on his motorbike, Hay Lin had begun flailing on the new skates. The boy had done his best to swerve out of her way, but the strap of Hay Lin's purple handbag had got caught on the back of his bike. Suddenly, Hay Lin had found herself taking flight behind Eric.

He had stopped immediately and offered his hand to pull her back to her feet after she'd fallen unceremoniously on her behind. Their attraction was immediate; he'd asked her to go out with him that very evening to count the shooting stars in a meteor shower.

They'd dated casually after that. But then Eric had become very busy with his studies. And as a Guardian, Hay Lin was constantly preoccupied with protecting the universe. At the moment, neither was very sure about the other's level of interest.

At the observatory, Eric gestured for Hay Lin to follow him across the lobby and large main hall. "Grandpa's waiting for us," he said.

"Come on. I'll take you to him."

Hay Lin followed, her hands behind her back, her smile fading slightly.

What a welcome, she thought with disappointment. I was hoping for something better, like . . . *May I have the honour of taking you to the party tomorrow?*

Eric's smile had faltered, too. Let's see, *May I please have the honour of taking you to the party tomorrow?* he said to himself, rehearsing silently as he led Hay Lin up the observatory's main marble staircase, then to a set of narrower, spiral stairs. Hmmm, thought Eric, "the honour"? Come on! Don't be so old-fashioned!

Continuing to eavesdrop, the Oracle tried not to smile.

Or, let's see . . . Eric said to himself. *Do you think I could go with you to the party?* No, that's wimpy.

Hay Lin followed Eric through a door marked PRIVATE. She stole glances at him, wishing he would ask her to the big school celebration being held in honour of Mrs. Rudolph. She waited and waited. But Eric appeared to be distracted, nervous, and lost in thought. The Oracle heard Hay Lin sigh heavily as she glanced around the space where Eric had taken her.

Star maps hung on the walls. A cluttered desk sat in the corner with a computer on top. Closer to the door stood a table and some chairs. And at the other end of the room was a large, raised platform, on top of which sat the observatory's huge telescope. One end was pointed at the sky through an opening in the vast domed roof above it. Eric's grandfather occupied the chair at the other end, deeply immersed in his work.

Hay Lin quickly realised that she'd seen this space before. It was the same room where she and Will had met Eric the first time they'd visited the observatory. She stole another glance at Eric. He still seemed nervous and uncomfortable.

Maybe he isn't that happy to see me after all, she thought, feeling doubt creep into her soul like a terrible chill.

The Oracle shook his head sadly. Not three feet away, Eric was actually saying all sorts of things to Hay Lin – in his mind.

How can I ask her out? the boy wondered. Maybe I could send her a note. A written invitation! That's it!

But by now, Hay Lin had completely given up. Oh, great! she wailed to herself. I'll have to ask him myself!

The Oracle sighed again as he observed Hay Lin and Eric struggling with their feelings.

"Imagine how many problems could be solved if only boys and girls could read each other's thoughts," the Oracle quietly mused. "But, who knows? With abilities like that in human hands, it's entirely likely even more problems would be created!"

THREE

"Are you two in the middle of a game of charades, or just a moment of embarrassed silence?" asked an amused male voice.

Hay Lin looked away from Eric to see Professor Lyndon walking towards them. He wore steel-framed glasses and a white lab coat. His bushy eyebrows and thick mustache were as silvery grey as the hair brushed back from his high forehead. His movements were slow and deliberate, and he leaned heavily on a cane.

"Oh . . . um . . . er . . ." Hay Lin stammered nervously.

The last time she'd seen the professor, he had been inside his unfinished planetarium in the observatory's basement. Eric had led her and Will down a narrow, dimly lit stairwell. But when he'd opened the door, he'd shown them a whole other world – literally.

An array of projectors and screens had made the entire basement of the vast observatory into a three-dimensional representation of the earth's solar system. Mercury, Venus, Earth, Mars, the asteroid belt, and about a billion stars all appeared real, as if they were spinning in orbits so close Hay Lin could reach out and touch them.

Hay Lin was in awe of Professor Zachary Lyndon. She'd been apprehensive about seeing him at first; meeting the relative of her crush had made her a little nervous. But he'd agreed to help with the diary, and that meant a lot to her.

Remembering her manners, Hay Lin cleared her throat and asked, "How are you, Mr. Lyndon?"

"Not good! Not good at all," replied the old astronomer. He ambled over to the small table where Hay Lin and Eric stood. Eric held a chair out for his grandfather, and Professor Lyndon slowly lowered himself into it.

"I looked over the diary you brought me," said the old man.

"Oh?" Hay Lin said, her eyes drawn to the leather-bound book in his hands. She hoped against hope that it would hold some answers for Will.

"It's extremely interesting, but terribly complicated," said Eric's grandfather. "To get to the bottom of it, I'll need more time."

Hay Lin's face fell. Between the disturbing fact that she was still hearing Nerissa's evil melody and Will's new and unusually negative attitude, Hay Lin didn't know how much more time they really had.

"Why such a disappointed look, young lady?" said the professor. "Rome wasn't built in a day, you know."

As Eric scratched his head, Hay Lin decided to press the professor into sharing *anything* he'd found, even the slightest detail. But before she could open her mouth to ask, the professor was already answering.

"This book contains an infinite wealth of information about an unknown star," he said. "A missing star."

Eric folded his arms. "Is there such a thing as a missing star, Grandpa?" he asked, sounding a little skeptical.

The professor slowly rose from the small table and crossed over to the raised platform where the observatory's huge telescope was mounted.

"This telescope has shown me all kinds of surprises, my boy," the professor replied. "According to this diary, the last time the star appeared was in the month of January, over ten years ago."

The professor sat down at the telescope and began to punch a series of coordinates into its keyboard. Hay Lin walked over and stood behind him.

"Between you and me, Hay Lin," the professor said without looking up, "I find it hard to believe that such a star exists."

Hay Lin clasped her hands together and took a deep breath. "Please, Mr. Lyndon . . . it's very important that my friends and I learn the truth."

"I see," replied the professor.

But how could he? thought Hay Lin. She certainly couldn't reveal the fact that she and her friends were Guardians, vested by the Oracle of Candracar with awesome powers to protect the universe from evil.

Well, actually, I *could* reveal it, she thought. But he'd probably tell Eric to get me some psychological help!

"All I can tell you, young lady, is that if that star is indeed out there . . . I'll find it." With that, the professor waved his hand and returned to the huge telescope, losing himself in his work.

Hay Lin realised she'd been dismissed. She turned to face Eric, but he quickly looked away, obviously embarrassed. Did he feel bad about the fact that his grandfather wasn't being more helpful with the diary? Or was he just nervous because he'd asked some *other* girl to the party already and was afraid Hay Lin would find out and get mad?

Eric was Hay Lin's first boyfriend ever. She wished she had had some experience to fall back on, like the other Guardians, especially Cornelia and Will. They'd been involved with boys for a while by then. They knew the score. Hay Lin didn't. She'd been the last one to even get a crush, which made her all the more clueless and all the more nervous to be facing Eric now, not knowing what to think or say in the awkward silence.

This is *stupid*, Hay Lin thought at last. I'm leaving.

Quickly, she strode to the observatory steps; then down, down, down she went until she reached the main hall. She heard Eric's footsteps following her, but he didn't say a word. Not one word! Not even as she breezed across the marble lobby, through the archway, and out into the chilly fall air.

Back on the busy sidewalks of Heatherfield, Hay Lin forced her mind off Eric. It wasn't hard. She was still worried about Will.

"I sure hope Professor Lyndon can help us discover the secret of that diary," Hay Lin murmured to herself as she trudged through the afternoon crowds.

It wasn't like Will to snap nastily at her the way she had earlier in the day. Hay Lin knew her friend was struggling, and she also knew about one of Will's deepest, darkest fears. Will was deeply worried that what had happened to Nerissa might happen to her.

Hay Lin could never see Will selfishly betraying her friends and turning evil. On the other hand, Hay Lin had to admit that evil did exist in the universe, and there was no telling how it might affect any one of the Guardians.

She thought of Nerissa. The evil crone had emerged from her tomb intent on gaining power and getting revenge on those who had put her there. Desperate to steal the Heart of Candracar, she'd begun assaulting the Guardians through their dreams, weakening them, exhausting them. But then the Guardians had fought her together, in the dream realm, and won.

Despite the fact that the Guardians had defeated the evil Nerissa, Hay Lin could still hear "Nerissa's Trill." That signature song had provided one of the first clues as to the fact that she was back.

That can't be good, thought Hay Lin. And it's a little frustrating being the only Guardian who can sense that something is very wrong!

That was another reason Hay Lin was anxious to solve the mystery of the diary. She was hoping Halinor's journal would give the Guardians an idea about how to protect themselves from evil forces like Nerissa.

I feel like we're close to something, Hay Lin thought. If Kadma gave us Halinor's diary, there must be a . . .

"Of course! Why didn't I think of it before?" Hay Lin cried, so loudly that a few people turned to look at her.

It was the appearance of the star that Hay Lin thought about as she walked along. According to the professor, the last time that had happened was over a decade ago. . . . That coincided more or less with the time when Will was born. That couldn't have been pure coincidence!

Hay Lin spied a phone booth across the street. She hurried over to it, pulling her phone card out of her pocket.

I've got to tell Will about it, she thought, dialing her best friend's cell phone. And I've got to do it now!

"Hello?" answered Will after a half dozen rings.

"Will! It's Hay Lin. I just talked to Professor Lyndon."

"Hay Lin, I'm sorry, but I just don't – "

"OK, OK! I know you don't want to talk about it," Hay Lin told her, "but I have some news that might interest you."

"All right," said Will with a sigh. "We're over at Petch. We'll wait for you inside."

Hay Lin hung up. She could hardly wait to

get to Will. If what the professor said was true, then Halinor must have been preparing to watch over and protect Will even before she was born!

"The shop's three blocks away," she murmured to herself. "It won't take me long. . . . But if I managed to get a ride from somebody, it'd take me even less time."

As Hay Lin walked towards the corner to cross the street, she noticed someone familiar riding by on a bicycle.

Great timing, she thought happily.

"Hey! Matt!" she cried.

Will's quasi boyfriend glanced up and smiled at Hay Lin, who was happy to see Matt for more reasons than just the possibility of getting a ride to Petch. Matt was someone who always made Will happy – and Hay Lin really wanted Will to be happy again.

After quickly asking Matt for a ride, she climbed on to his bike and found herself wishing Eric Lyndon were as relaxed and cool as Matt Olsen. Her smile faltered a bit as she remembered how disappointing her observatory visit had been.

Eric was getting more awkward around her,

not less. That couldn't be good, thought Hay Lin. And he hadn't even asked her to the party!

Whatever, she thought as Matt took off down the street. Until I met Eric, I'd never let a stupid boy ruin my day. And I'm not about to start now!

FOUR

"Happy?" asked Will.

Yes, thank you very much, Cornelia thought. She smiled at Will, pleased about the phone call that had just ended. Thank goodness Will had held her temper with Hay Lin instead of snapping at her as she had earlier that day. Even better, Will had actually invited Hay Lin to join their shopping expedition.

Will shrugged. "So this way, I'll make up for what I said earlier at school."

Cornelia nodded her approval. "Come on," she said, walking out of the frame shop. She led the way to her favourite clothing boutique.

Petch had a lot of great clothes – some classic, some trendy. Cornelia checked out the new inventory and waved Will over, to see what she thought of an extremely cool robin's-egg blue blouse with bell-shaped sleeves and a lace collar.

"This is cute," said Cornelia. "I bet it would look great on you."

Will grabbed the sleeve and read the tag. "Yeah," she said, "but it's a bit too pricey for me."

Cornelia nodded.

"I'll have to ask for a raise in my allowance," Will joked. "Do your folks give you an allowance?"

"Not really," said Cornelia, with a shrug. "Whenever I have to go shopping I just ask for money."

Cornelia was going to suggest that they look at the closeout racks for some good discounts when a funny look came over Will's face.

A moment later, Will turned towards the saleswoman who was behind them folding sweaters. "Huh?" she said, as if the woman had just spoken to her.

But the saleswoman didn't even look up from her work.

That's really odd, thought Cornelia. What is Will's deal?

Just then, Cornelia noticed a cute guy on a bicycle pulling up in front of the store. "Hey! Look who's here," she said, moving to the plate-glass window.

"Wh – who said that?" Will blurted out.

Cornelia turned around to see Will's head whipping from side to side. Will was still standing near the saleswoman who was folding sweaters.

"Will?" Cornelia said. She didn't like the look on Will's face. There was something unsettling, as if her friend had suddenly been plagued with dark thoughts. Cornelia remembered what Will had said earlier, about the Heart weighing on her, making her feel exhausted and negative and down.

Well, this should cheer her up, Cornelia thought, looking out the window. "Come see who's here," she called.

Will shuffled up to the picture window and stared at the scene taking place on the sidewalk. Her eyes widened.

Cornelia expected her to start bubbling over with chatter about her boyfriend's showing up.

Will Vandom and Matt Olsen really did make the perfect couple. Both were big into helping animals. Will took care of a little dormouse she'd rescued, and Matt worked at his grandfather's pet shop. They liked listening to the same kind of music, too. In fact, as Cornelia remembered, Will had first started crushing on Matt when she heard him singing and playing lead guitar with his band, Cobalt Blue, at a Hallowe'en party.

A lot had happened since then, thought Cornelia. She had fallen in love, too, just like Will. But at least Will had been smart enough to fall for a guy there on earth!

Cornelia's boyfriend, Caleb, was from Metamoor. She'd met him while the Guardians were fighting evil in his world. He'd been fighting, too, leading a rebellion against Prince Phobos, who had stolen the throne from his sister, Elyon, the rightful heir of Meridian. Caleb, along with the Guardians, had helped to stop Phobos.

Just the memory of Caleb melted Cornelia. At the moment, he was far away, in another world, and in pretty bad shape, too. His struggle with the evil Nerissa had left him stripped of much of his identity. But he was recovering now, under the Oracle's care. Cornelia thought of Caleb every morning and every night. She sent her most loving thoughts up to him in Candracar, hoping he could hear them within the healing room of the Temple.

Cornelia watched as Matt stopped his bicycle on the sidewalk in front of Petch.

Hay Lin hopped off the bike's handlebars and turned to say something to Matt. She must have said something funny, because they both started to laugh.

Cornelia smiled, thinking that a little laughter was exactly what Will needed at that moment. But when she looked, she saw that Will wasn't laughing. Instead, she was frowning, then glancing back at that same saleswoman again.

"What are you saying?" Will whispered.

"I didn't say anything," Cornelia replied.

"I wasn't talking to you," snapped Will.

"What? Will, are you OK?" Cornelia tried to put an arm around Will's shoulders as she had in front of the print and frame store. But Will violently pulled away.

"Why is Matt flirting with her like that?" she whispered, her voice a mixture of pain and anger as she pointed to the window. "Like he doesn't know Hay Lin's my friend!"

Cornelia couldn't believe her ears. "But Will, they're just kidding around. There's nothing wrong with that."

"If there's nothing wrong, then you talk to her," said Will. "I'm leaving. I really don't feel like arguing!"

"Will what's got into you? Wait!" Cornelia cried, but Will was already rushing towards the back of the store.

"Is there a back door, please?" Will asked the cashier.

"Will!" Cornelia tried again, but her only answer was the slam of the back door.

"What's going on, Cornelia?" Hay Lin called.

Cornelia turned to find the air Guardian standing in the shop's front entrance. Sighing, Cornelia shook her head. "I really don't understand her."

"*Unh!*" Hay Lin suddenly cried, holding her head as if she'd just received a sharp blow.

"Hay Lin!" Cornelia rushed over to put a strong arm around her friend.

Whoa, thought Cornelia. First Will and now Hay Lin! "What's got into *you* now? Are you feeling OK?" she asked.

"That music, Cornelia!" Hay Lin replied, leaning her slight form against the earth Guardian.

"What music?" Cornelia asked.

"For . . . for a moment I heard 'Nerissa's Trill' again," said Hay Lin, still holding her head.

Oh, no, Cornelia thought. She led Hay Lin outside for some fresh air. "Are you sure?"

"That's what it sounded like," Hay Lin insisted as they stepped on to the wide concrete sidewalk. "It's like that tune is still echoing through my head."

Cornelia knew exactly why Hay Lin was so freaked out. Nerissa was a tough enemy. It had been Cornelia who had figured out how to defeat her in the first place, but it hadn't been easy.

After the Guardians had suffered weeks of assault in Nerissa's nightmares, Cornelia had suggested that they try to fight the evil sorceress all together, while in the dream. During a slumber party at Cornelia's apartment, the girls had gone to sleep and entered the same dream together. Cornelia remembered how they had managed to trap Nerissa in the Heart. The former Guardian had hurled all of her powers against the surface of the crystal, causing her to disappear in a blinding flash of light. The girls had assumed that she'd finally been destroyed.

Yet now, Cornelia thought, Will is freaking out, and Hay Lin says she can still hear the old crone's song. Is it possible that Nerissa herself is gone but that her dark powers are still hanging around, like some sort of evil exhaust fumes?

If that was what was really happening, Cornelia was forced to admit, she had no clue how to fix the problem.

I may be a shopaholic, she thought, but I don't know any boutiques in Heatherfield that carry Nerissa Begone perfume!

Still, the Guardians couldn't afford to take those warnings lightly, and Cornelia knew it.

"Why did Will leave?" Hay Lin asked, looking around.

"She's in a weird mood today," Cornelia replied. "Listen, there's something about her that's worrying me. . . . Maybe we should meet up to talk about all this tomorrow, before the party. *Without* Will."

Hay Lin quickly nodded in agreement.

"Well, let's get going then," said Cornelia, pointing Hay Lin in the direction of the Silver Dragon restaurant. The way the girl was trembling, Cornelia intended to make absolutely sure she got home all right.

"And on the way," Cornelia added, "you can tell me what you found out at the observatory."

"All right," said Hay Lin, "but do you think Will is going to be OK?"

"I think so," Cornelia replied. "Let's hope that a goodnight's sleep will bring her to her senses."

FIVE

For the rest of the day, Will felt completely numb. After barely a few bites of dinner, she headed into her bedroom, changed into her favourite striped pyjamas, and sat in the dark, staring out the window.

Bedtime could be a tricky business, Will decided. When things were going well, it felt good to climb under her comfy froggy blankets and let dreams come. But when things were going badly, the last thing she wanted to do was close her eyes and let the inevitable nightmares start.

On the other hand, she thought, after what she'd been through that day, a nightmare might have been a relief.

First, the elegant clerk in the frame

and print shop had whispered dark thoughts into Will's mind. And then the saleswoman in Petch had started doing it.

The Petch incident was worse, Will decided. She could still hear the hiss of the woman's voice in her head.

"Cornelia is a lot luckier than you, kid," the woman had whispered after Will admitted she couldn't afford the pretty blue blouse Cornelia had picked out.

Then, as Will had watched Matt flirt with Hay Lin through the window, the same saleswoman had given her a terrible warning: *"Don't trust those who say they're your friends, Will. Don't trust anyone!"*

That was when Will had lost it and run out of the store. She'd circled back to the front of the store to see if Matt was still there, only to overhear Cornelia talking to Hay Lin on the sidewalk outside.

"Maybe we should meet up to talk about it tomorrow, before the party," Cornelia had said. *"Without Will."*

Without Will, Will repeated to herself. *Without Will.* . . . She drew her knees up and hugged them to her chest. The saleswoman was right, she thought. I can't trust any of my friends any more.

"In bed already?" asked Will's mother, stepping into the shadowy bedroom and breaking the silence.

"Yeah, Mom," Will replied. "I'm going to sleep. I'm pretty tired."

"You didn't say a thing during dinner. Everything all right?" Mrs. Vandom asked gently. She sat down on the bed.

The genuine concern in her mother's voice made Will's eyes fill up with tears. "Not really," she admitted, dropping her chin on to her knees.

Mrs. Vandom moved closer to stroke Will's shaggy red hair. "What's wrong, sweetheart?" she asked softly.

Will sniffled and wiped her eyes. "You know when everything goes wrong, no matter what you do?"

"Of course," said Will's mother. "I've been there lots of times. But I'm still hanging in there."

Will looked up into her mother's eyes. The two of them hadn't always had the best relationship. There'd been several times when Will had felt as though there were a million miles between her and her mother – though she'd sometimes felt that way about everyone else, too, to be honest.

When the two of them had moved to Heatherfield, they had proceeded to fight 24-7. Then things had got even worse, when her mother had started dating Mr. Collins, one of Will's teachers at Sheffield. Will had become so angry and embarrassed she hadn't even wanted to speak to her mother. But over time, things had got better between them. Slowly, Will had stopped seeing her mum as the enemy.

When you're a Guardian, Will realised, you find out there are actually a lot worse things in the world than being told to clean your room and observe your curfew.

Mrs. Vandom squeezed her daughter's shoulder. "The trick is not to let the bad things get you down," she said.

Will wiped a tear away from her cheek. "Does that really work?"

Mrs. Vandom shrugged. "It doesn't always work, but I think that it's worth giving it a shot. . . . Convinced?"

"Not really," said Will. "But thanks for trying. I'll sleep on it tonight. Maybe tomorrow I'll have changed my mind."

"Sweet dreams, then, Will," said Mrs. Vandom. As Will released her knees and stretched out, her mom leaned close and kissed her on the cheek.

Will smiled. She'd been feeling really alone that night, as if she hadn't had a friend left in the world. She was suddenly glad, *really* glad, that her mother had come in to check on her. "Goodnight, Mum."

As Mrs. Vandom walked out of the room, Will's dormouse jumped onto the bed near Will's feet.

"Good thing I have her to talk to," Will confided to the chipper critter. "Come on over here." The furry little animal scampered up to her, swished its bushy tail, and blinked its round, black eyes. Will turned on to her side and gently scratched behind the animal's tiny ears.

"*Rrrttt?*" said the dormouse.

"Oh, of course," Will replied with a laugh. "I couldn't manage without you, either, my little friend!"

Will still remembered the day she'd rescued the animal from the flame-haired creep Uriah and his scruffy crew of greasy, low–I.Q. slacker jerks. They had been trying to trap the little dormouse so they could shove it into someone's locker as a prank. But the clever dormouse had chomped down on Uriah's finger and got away.

Before the bully could catch the little animal again, Will had scooped it up in her arms. Then she'd yelled at the top of her lungs at Uriah and his pinheaded followers until they'd had no choice but to walk away.

That was when it happened – Matt walked up to her.

Will closed her eyes, picturing Matt's tall, lanky form, his strong jaw dusted with scruffy stubble, his shaggy brown hair, and his long-lashed eyes. He always looked cool and relaxed. She loved how he'd helped her with the dormouse that day, telling her all about its habits and what it should eat. He'd even wrapped it in his orange sweater for her to take home.

Even now, Will's pulse raced at the memory of their first meeting – how he'd given her his number and flirted with her. Her heart had melted when he'd flashed his cute smile at her. But that memory suddenly changed in Will's mind, replacing itself with the image of Matt standing in front of Petch today, flirting with Hay Lin.

Arrrrgggghhh!

Will flopped around on her mattress, agitated.

So many things had happened lately, she realised. Too many. . . . In her shoes, anyone else would've gone nuts already, she thought. And maybe that was just what was happening to her.

Doubt can really torment a person, Will thought, staring at the curtains fluttering in the chilly night breeze. Just one whisper of doubt leads to another and another . . . then they start piling up until you feel as though you're being buried alive!

Will shivered, remembering Nerissa's punishment. The Oracle and the Elders of Candracar had sentenced her to be imprisoned inside a volcanic tomb.

"Nerissa had been a Keeper," she murmured in the moonlit room. "She had been good once, too. But she changed. Could the same thing happen to me?"

Tormented by her deepest fear, she felt the Heart inside her growing hot and unbelievably heavy.

Will squeezed her eyes shut and breathed deeply, trying to force the negative thoughts and feelings out of her head. She tried not to let the bad things get her down, just as her mother had advised her.

"Those weird voices that were talking to me earlier today," she murmured, "maybe I *didn't* hear them, after all. Maybe I just imagined that I heard them. . . ."

Suddenly, however, she heard that saleswoman's voice in her head again. *"Don't trust those who say they're your friends. Don't trust anyone!"*

Will pulled a pillow over her head, as if that could drown out the voice.

I . . . I need to spend some time alone from now on, Will couldn't help thinking. I don't want to . . . to have to *trust* anyone any more. The world is too full of phony friends . . . people who smile at you but don't mean it. . . . Maybe Cornelia's one of them, and Hay Lin, too . . . and all the others!

Will yanked the pillow away from her face

and violently sat up on the mattress. The dormouse jumped down to find a safe spot on the carpet.

I've made up my mind, she thought. As of tomorrow, lots of things are going to change. And this is the best moment to do it. Nerissa isn't a threat any more, and everything is quiet in Candracar. So, before some new danger brings W.I.T.C.H. together again, I'll have to solve all of my problems . . . alone.

SIX

From a place in Candracar, Yan Lin observed an ethereal image of her beloved granddaughter's bedroom.

Books and drawings were scattered about. Paintbrushes, pencils, and pens were strewn across a small craft table. Leg warmers had taken up residence in one corner, a skirt and pair of tights in another. Bright yellow goggles hung precariously over a chair. And an open messenger bag lay half emptied of its contents beneath her desk.

Tsk, tsk, tsk, thought the old woman, cataloging the disarray. I see some things haven't changed a bit since I left! Of course, I always did tell my granddaughter that a messy room indicated a creative mind. And there are so many good memories here . . . so many . . .

For countless evenings, Yan Lin had perched herself on that very bed in that very room. While Han Lin's parents were running the Silver Dragon restaurant downstairs, Yan Lin had watched over Hay Lin in their apartment upstairs. Every night, she would tuck the little girl in and tell her stories about ancient heroes.

Yan Lin still remembered the warm and wonderful scents that had risen from the busy kitchen below – sizzling beef and peanut oil, garlic and ginger, fragrant tea.

At this moment, however, the dining room was empty, and the city beyond it quiet and dark.

Hay Lin's long, loose hair spilled across her white pillow in dark streaks that resembled streams of black paint. Her almond-shaped eyes were closed in a deep sleep. Now, thought Yan Lin, it is time for my beloved granddaughter to dream. . . .

"Hello, Hay Lin," called Yan Lin.

The young girl stirred beneath her blankets.

She turned over on her mattress and rubbed her eyes with small, delicate fists.

"Grandma? Is that you?" Hay Lin asked. Sitting up, she regarded the old woman in her dazzling white robe. "What . . . what are you doing here?"

"I've come to see you," said Yan Lin. "But I don't have much time. I just wanted to remind you about our little riddle."

Yan Lin bowed her head. The walls of Hay Lin's cluttered bedroom slowly dissolved. The bed was now hovering in an open field. Trees, grass, and flowers stretched to a blue horizon with clouds reminiscent of the celestial beauty of Candracar.

"Riddle?" asked Hay Lin. She jumped down from her hovering bed into the grassy field and walked towards her grandmother. Her oversize nightshirt fluttered in the breeze.

Yan Lin slowly lifted one robed arm and gestured to an enormous oak tree in the field behind her. "On a stormy day, which is stronger?" Yan Lin asked her granddaughter. "The oak tree or the reed?"

Hay Lin considered the question for a few moments. She regarded the old oak, towering over the large field. Its trunk was more than three feet thick, and it stood about fifty feet high. Around the tree grew clusters of strawlike reeds.

"I'd say the oak," Hay Lin replied. "But that wouldn't be the right answer, would it?" she asked doubtfully.

"I, too, answered that way when I was your age," said Yan Lin. "And many years later, by acting like an oak, I made the biggest mistake of my life."

Yan Lin raised her hands, and the slight breeze in the air became a brisk wind. *Whooosh!* In seconds, the powerful wind grew even stronger. It gusted faster and faster until it blew with hurricane strength.

Hay Lin's loose, long hair lifted on the wind, whipping about her head like wild black tentacles. She turned away from the unrelenting force, trying in vain to shield her face from its raw intensity.

"Under mighty gusts of wind, the oak resists without bending," shouted Yan Lin over the wind's roar, her long, white hair fluttering around her wrinkled face like a silver halo. "But sooner or later, it breaks . . ."

C-r-r-a-a-a-a-c-k!

The relentless assault of the wind had caused the old oak's trunk to crack and splinter like a toothpick. As the terrible wind died down, the old Guardian walked over to the cluster of reeds, still intact at the base of the broken oak.

". . . While the reed bows gently, so that it never breaks," Yan Lin quietly finished. She brushed the thin, delicate plants with her wrinkled hand, then turned to face her granddaughter.

"I've returned only to tell you this, Hay Lin," said Yan Lin. Of course, she *wanted* to tell her granddaughter much more. But it was not permitted.

Long ago, when Yan Lin had served as a Guardian with Nerissa, she had never doubted the beautiful, intelligent Keeper of the Heart. Nor had she suspected that Nerissa was capable of evil. But Nerissa *was* capable of it. She'd changed into a monster, someone who spurned the help and good intentions of others. That truth was undeniable.

Yan Lin feared that the same thing was happening all over again – to Will. And if Will chose to turn against her best friends, Hay Lin might be in terrible danger.

The Oracle would not allow Yan Lin to say anything to Hay Lin regarding her specific doubts about Will. The future was a shifting, uncertain thing, after all, dependent on millions of choices by millions of beings. Will and her fellow Guardians would always remain free to choose their own paths.

But the Oracle had allowed Yan Lin this one admonition. It would not make much sense to her granddaughter now. But in time, Yan Lin knew, if Hay Lin remembered this lesson, it could save her life.

If only I had received a similar warning, Yan Lin thought, perhaps things would have turned out differently.

Yan Lin regarded her little Hay Lin, standing in her field of dreams. Her beautiful dark eyes were filled with a combination of awe and utter confusion.

Yan Lin smiled and pulled Hay Lin into a close hug. The familiar warmth of the little girl filled the old woman with joy. She could sense Hay Lin's vitality. She could feel her deep love, her unwavering trust.

"I can't talk to you for long," Yan Lin said, even as she began to pull her awareness back into the ether of the cosmos, back to everywhere and nowhere. "So remember," she advised her, "*never* let your memories slip away."

"Wait, Grandma!" Hay Lin called.

Yan Lin's image gradually paled into a transparent silhouette.

"Please, Grandma!" cried Hay Lin. "Stay here with me a little longer. . . ."

The sorrowful longing in Hay Lin's voice sent a bittersweet pain through Yan Lin's heart. Leaving her little granddaughter again was not easy. But Yan Lin had come to terms with an important lesson long ago. The universe, while granting many blessings, also required sacrifice.

Because Yan Lin understood and accepted that universal truth, she had been allowed to enter Candracar. Now she would do all she could to see that one day her own little Hay Lin would also find a place with the Oracle in the great Temple.

Trilee, trilee, trilee, lee, lee . . . Triloo, triloo, trilooooo!

"Oh, no!" Hay Lin cried, putting her hands over her ears. "The music!"

As Yan Lin faded from Hay Lin's dreams, she, too, heard the familiar, flute-like sound. And she knew at once what the evil melody portended.

"It's 'Nerissa's Trill'!" Hay Lin cried. "There's no mistaking it. I can hear it distinctly. She's still here!"

From far away, Yan Lin watched her grand-daughter run across the field where she'd left her. The girl was trying to get back to her hovering bed, which began to rise higher and higher into the sky. Hay Lin grabbed the dangling bedsheet and tried desperately to pull herself up.

"She's here!" Hay Lin called. "Grandma, she's listening to us! We're too close. Let's go! Hurry!"

Yan Lin closed her eyes and concentrated. In the next instant, Hay Lin was no longer dreaming.

Thump!

"Eeeek!" cried Hay Lin, opening her eyes to find that she had rolled off her bed and on to her cluttered bedroom floor.

"It can't be," Hay Lin whispered, rubbing her eyes. "It can't be . . . but now I know it's true."

Hmmm, thought Yan Lin, observing her granddaughter. It seems my visit has emboldened my old enemy. Good. Now Hay Lin knows the truth. It may not be a pleasant truth, but it is good that she knows it.

Climbing back onto her bed, Hay Lin's eyes were wide with fear. "It's true," she murmured, "Nerissa's alive. . . . She's alive."

SEVEN

Through the centuries of imprisonment inside Mount Thanos, Nerissa's form had been completely ravaged. Her blue eyes had turned into hollow black pits. Her teeth, once straight and perfect, had become rotten and broken. Her lustrous dark hair had dried and changed to the consistency of filthy straw. And her velvety skin had turned into something like brittle parchment.

Year after year, she'd listened to the churning waves of the frosty tide, the violent bubbling of the molten lava. She'd seethed and hated and cursed those who had trapped her, vowing to destroy them all if she ever got the chance.

And then, after what had felt like

an eternity, she had got one.

Fate had allowed the dark sorceress to emerge from the desolate prison of volcanic fire and polar ice in which she'd spent so many years. Using her powerful magic, she'd regenerated her exotic beauty. Once again, her hair had become long and lustrous, her skin soft, her form voluptuous. Once again, her eyes were bluer than the Arctic Ocean. And her hatred was more venomous than ever.

Inside her craggy cavern, Nerissa now sat upon her makeshift throne, looking as stunning as she had when she'd been a young, vital Keeper of the Heart. Even her gown appeared new again, the long burgundy velvet draping itself over the jagged rocks below. A few feet away, her three servants, Tridart, Ember, and Shagon, stood obediently awaiting their mistress's command.

"The girl doesn't seem to believe you've been defeated," said Tridart. He was the iceman, his head bald and smooth, his armour crystalline. Nerissa had used her evil power to carve him out of the frozen landscape around the volcanic mountain.

"The little brat's right," Nerissa snarled at

her servant. Using her dark magic, she had been spying on Hay Lin, watching her while she slept, hearing her fearful cries that Nerissa was now *alive!*

Well, thought Nerissa, *I am!* "Will may have defeated me in the world of dreams," she told the three servants at her feet, "but she didn't defeat me completely. I'm still around."

Beside Tridart stood Ember, the winged female with skin of black ash and hair of red fire. She'd been created from Mount Thanos's boiling lava.

From the confused look on her servant's face, Nerissa could see that Ember did not understand what had happened to her.

Well, my little hothead, Nerissa thought, I fought the Guardians in their collective dream. And I lost badly. So I can no longer enter their world of dreams to torment them. That ability is lost to me.

A surprise attack is essential now, Nerissa decided. Those little Guardians believe I was destroyed. *Good.* I want them to go on believing it . . . right up to the moment I spring my trap!

Nerissa hated to admit it, but her battle

against the Guardians had been exceptionally draining. Taking a little rest while she recovered from her defeat had enabled her to gather her strength and wits for another assault. However, this next one was going to be completely different from the first. This time she would not lose.

"I will return," she'd long ago warned the Oracle and the Congregation of Candracar, "and you will regret having stood in my way!" Now, at long last, she was ready to live up to her words.

I must have the Heart again, she told herself. Once that precious crystal is back in my possession, I shall combine it with the copy of the powers of the five Guardians, which I obtained from the Herald of Candracar. Then the Oracle, the Congregation, those tiresome Guardians, and the entire universe will see a force the likes of which they've never before imagined!

The only possible snag in Nerissa's perfect plan was the persistent probing of the current air Guardian.

"Hay Lin is like her grandmother," Nerissa told her servants. "There was a special bond between Yan Lin and me . . . and certain bonds never break."

That must be why the girl keeps hearing my trill, she thought. It's like some kind of cosmic alarm inherited from her grandmother. A warning to her that I'm close by. That's how she figured out I'm still alive.

"Then you'd better stay away from her, Nerissa," warned Shagon.

Of all her servants, Shagon was Nerissa's absolute favourite. Clad in his characteristic sky-blue armour, the brawny warrior stood with Tridart and Ember at the foot of Nerissa's rough throne, waiting to do her evil bidding. Unlike her other servants, however, who had been carved from nonhuman elements, Shagon had once been an actual human being. Nerissa had plucked a wayward geologist from Mount Thanos's volcanic rim, then enthralled him, using her powerful magic. Since then, he had risen to become one of the most dangerous weapons in her plot for revenge against the Congregation.

Shagon's thick blonde mane framed a face as pale and blank as a puppet's. Using her own centuries-old rage, Nerissa had rigged him to thrive on the emotion of hate. Unfortunately, however, he was still a flesh-and-blood human underneath it all. And his impudent human tendency to think for himself sometimes surfaced in the form of spoken opinions – a habit that Nerissa did not approve of at all.

How tiresome to have to explain myself to a servant, Nerissa thought in disgust. "I know what I have to do, Shagon!" she screeched, standing up on her rocky throne and pointing her dark staff at him in warning. "We have nothing to fear. The other girls feel safe. They won't take Hay Lin's warning signals too seriously."

Shagon, Tridart, and Ember all nodded obediently. They knew better than to anger Nerissa any further.

"We'll keep working on Will," Nerissa continued.

She stepped down off her throne. Pacing inside the cavern, she barely noticed that her velvet gown was trailing along the rocky earth. It narrowly missed the lava pools that sizzled like meat on a grill as icicles dropped into them from the ceiling of the cavern.

"Thanks to your hints of hate, Shaggy, I've instilled doubt in the Keeper of the Heart," said Nerissa. Her blue eyes glowed with satisfaction at the memory of the effect that the two Heatherfield saleswomen had had on Will. "Those creatures are totally unaware that they're under your control!"

How delightful it had been to see Shagon speaking through that saleswoman at the frame shop, thought Nerissa. How entertaining to see a woman so elegant, so refined, delivering such deliciously hateful thoughts and sowing doubts between friends. The evil sorceress smiled as she recalled the wicked words: *she doesn't seem to care much about what you're going through, does she, Will?*

Then came the second saleswoman, at the trendy clothing store. Shagon had been even more effective channelling his hate through her. *Don't trust those who say they're your friends, Will. Don't trust anyone!*

Those final remarks had actually sent the little red-headed Guardian running out the back door, Nerissa recalled with glee. Her plan was working perfectly.

"I can't just *take* the Heart of Candracar from her," she reminded her servants, "but at the end of all this, I won't even need to. It will be Will herself who delivers it into my hands!"

Shagon nodded obediently at his mistress, eager to believe her, and more than willing to follow her.

"It will be Will who opens the doors to Candracar for me," Nerissa vowed, "and this will happen only after she has defeated her dear *friends*. . . . Ha-ha-ha!"

EIGHT

The elderly maths teacher sat down in her favourite pink living-room chair. Clad in her comfy pink robe, Mrs. Rudolph lifted her slippered feet onto a footrest and pressed the phone to her ear.

Ring, ring, ring . . .

"Hello?" said a woman's voice on the other end of the line.

"Hello. May I speak to Taranee, please?" asked Mrs. Rudolph.

Of the five Guardians, Taranee is my very best student, thought the maths teacher, pushing her large, square glasses up on her nose. If anyone can figure out a solution to my problem, I'm sure

Taranee can! At least, I hope she can. . . .

"Taranee!" she heard the woman shout on the other end of the line.

That must be Judge Cook, Taranee's mother, thought Mrs. Rudolph. Then she heard a "Yeah?" from far away.

"Phone call. Somebody wants to speak with you!" cried the woman on the other end of the line.

There was a short pause, and then Taranee's mom spoke again. "It's ten o'clock!" she told Taranee in a scolding voice. "After nine-thirty at night, people shouldn't be calling others up. It's not polite."

"If everyone had a mother like you," Taranee answered in a wry voice, "the world wouldn't be so chaotic."

Mrs. Rudolph stifled a laugh on her end of the line. Very good answer, she thought. Then again, that was just like her best maths student: logical *and* witty!

There was silence for another moment. While Mrs. Rudolph continued to wait, she heard two adult voices talking – one male, one female. She assumed they belonged to Taranee's parents.

"Lionel," said Judge Cook, "since when has our daughter had a sense of humour?"

"*Hmmm,*" replied Taranee's father. "Must be since you two started spending *less* time together!"

"Oh, very funny," Judge Cook answered back.

Mrs. Rudolph was still chuckling softly to herself when Taranee's bright voice came on the line.

"Hello?" the girl said.

"Taranee," Mrs. Rudolph began. "Sorry I'm calling so late. Were you sleeping?"

"Oh, no, Mrs. Rudolph, I was reading," Taranee replied.

"Well, I still haven't thanked you for the lovely gesture of you and your classmates. But actually, there was something else I wanted to speak to you about."

Mrs. Rudolph paused for a moment trying to decide how to introduce the next delicate subject. "My retirement from teaching is . . . more than it seems."

"That's what I thought, Mrs. Rudolph," said Taranee right away. Then she lowered her voice. "Now that Meridian is free again, are you going back to your world?"

Mrs. Rudolph closed her eyes and smiled, pleased and relieved that Taranee understood why she had called.

The five Guardians were the only beings on earth who knew the truth about their maths teacher: that her real teeth looked more like jagged, razor-sharp fangs; that underneath her greying blonde hair were red dreadlocks. Beneath her wrinkling human skin were brown and green scales. Her actual nose was more like a snout. Her real ears were long and crooked, almost like antlers, while her real eyes were bulgy and glowed red. Her hands were more like claws, and her feet were really giant paws with three floppy toes each and a thumb-like digit on the heel.

Mrs. Rudolph still remembered the day that two of the Guardians had sneaked into her house to spy on her, thinking that she was an evil creature from Meridian. From their hiding place, Irma and Hay Lin had watched in horror as their short, plump, grandmotherly maths teacher transformed herself into an enormous, otherworldly creature.

"Watch out!" Irma had screamed. "She's a monster from Metamoor."

Mrs. Rudolph might have looked like a monster, but the truth was she never intended to harm a soul. She'd come through an open portal, travelling to Earth to escape the terrible war in her world.

All of that terrible chaos had been settled, of course. The Guardians had bravely helped the rebels defeat the evil Prince Phobos, who had terrorised all of Metamoor. Now Elyon, the rightful queen, sat on the throne in the capital city of Meridian. All was well again in Mrs. Rudolph's world.

Of course, while the war was going on, Mrs. Rudolph had tried hard to keep her identity a secret. After Hay Lin and Irma had first discovered who she really was, they'd alerted Will, and the three had chased Mrs. Rudolph back to Metamoor through the portal in her attic. Then the girls had used their powers to close that portal tight.

But Mrs. Rudolph found her way back to the earth again by way of another portal that had opened up in Heatherfield. She'd explained everything to the Guardians – that she had simply wanted to find some peace and security on earth and never intended to harm a soul – and especially not any of the Guardians.

They had agreed to keep her secret. And as far as Mrs. Rudolph knew, they had never breathed a word about the fact that a being from another world was teaching algebra at Sheffield Institute.

Now that she was retiring, however, the otherworldly teacher had a problem. How was she going to return to her world? To keep the earth safe, the Guardians had closed every last portal she'd ever known about.

"Unfortunately, with the portals closed now," Mrs. Rudolph told Taranee, "I can't go back unless you help me. I have to ask you for a special favour."

"Don't worry," Taranee replied with warmth in her voice. "We'll take care of everything. We can talk it over tomorrow night."

The dear girl, thought Mrs. Rudolph as she said goodnight, rose from her chair, and hung up the phone. I'll miss her and her friends so much when I'm back in Metamoor.

She moved across the wood-plank floor of her large old house. As she exited the living room, she flipped off the light.

But I'm certain that they'll come to visit me

once in a while, she decided as she began to climb the staircase. That's what always happens with old, retired teachers. And their friend Elyon is there, too, so there is even more incentive to visit.

K – dump!

Mrs. Rudolph stopped in her tracks. "Huh? What was that?" she whispered. "Is . . . is someone there?"

She turned around very cautiously and quietly went back down the stairs.

Click!

She flipped the lights back on and glanced around the living room and hallway.

"Nobody," she muttered to herself.

Shaking her head, she headed for the staircase once more. "I could have sworn I heard something. . . ."

Just then, Mrs. Rudolph sensed a strange heaviness draping itself over her, like an invisible shroud. It was an uncomfortable feeling. At the same moment, she could swear she'd seen a bizarre image reflected in her hallway mirror. She rubbed her eyes and looked at the image again. It looked like a gigantic warrior!

Clothed in sky-blue armour, he was brawny,

with arms as thick as tree trunks. A shaggy mane of blonde hair framed his strange face, which appeared as blank and white as a mask. He seemed to be coming straight towards her.

How strange indeed, Mrs. Rudolph thought, as she saw the creature lift his huge, clawlike hands. He looked just like a puppeteer preparing to pull the strings on a brand-new marionette.

NINE

Weird, thought Cornelia as she walked across Sheffield's lawn, I'm getting that déjà vu feeling all over again.

In the dark of night, the bright lights shone through the tall windows of the school, casting islands of illumination throughout the shadowy quad. Torches flickered along the stone walkway. Kids flowed, laughing and talking, across the school grounds, then up the stairs to the entrance of the gym. Outfitted in colourful dresses, long skirts, leather jackets, and thick turtlenecks, they moved in small and large groups.

There was a buzz in the chilly fall air. It was that electric feeling that charges the atmosphere before a party is about to begin. It reminded Cornelia of what had taken place there a little over a year before. On that night, the night of Sheffield's annual Hallowe'en party, the lives of the Guardians had suddenly changed.

The five girls had been together at that time, but not yet *united*. Then Cedric and Vathek, evil beings from Metamoor, had strolled in, their monstrous forms blending right in with the students' Hallowe'en costumes. Later that night, all five members of W.I.T.C.H. had dreamed of the Heart of Candracar. The next day, Hay Lin's grandmother had told them the truth about their powers and presented Will with the actual glowing object that was the Heart.

Cornelia recalled how truly freaked she'd been at that moment. There was no way she'd wanted to believe what Hay Lin's grandmother was telling them.

It's hard to believe I ever felt differently than I do now, she thought. I've changed so much. It's almost like remembering the feelings of a different person.

But eventually Cornelia had embraced her Guardian powers and responsibilities. And over the last year, she'd been through a lot with her fellow Guardians. There had been the battle over Metamoor; the struggle to help Elyon regain her throne; the harrowing transformation of Caleb into a flower and back to human form again; the treachery of Luba; and, finally, the evil assault of Nerissa.

Now another party was about to begin in the very same place where the other one had been. All five Guardians were going to be there, just as they had the year before. At first glance, the whole scene might have looked like a repeat of the previous year's performance. But something was definitely different. Now, W.I.T.C.H. was united, a seasoned group that had been through a battle and back again. And Cornelia was no longer unsure of herself. More than ever, she appreciated the duty to make certain that each member of W.I.T.C.H. protected the world and one another from evil.

Adjusting her long, teal wrap around her shoulders, Cornelia glanced worriedly around the lawn. There was no sign of the other Guardians outside, so she climbed the steps to the gym, her long taffeta skirt rustling as she moved.

A cluster of kids and teachers were fussing around the refreshment table. They were filling punch bowls, dumping ice into big tubs filled with soda cans, and laying out countless plates of cupcakes and biscuits. At the other end of the large space, Matt Olsen was going through a sound check with Cobalt Blue. *"Check, check!"* reverberated through the gym.

Kids were still arriving and gathering inside, but Cornelia hadn't yet seen any members of W.I.T.C.H. She wondered where her friends could be. Frustrated, she headed out of the gym. She walked down the main hall, but there was still no sign of her friends.

As she walked towards the exit of the building, she heard some familiar voices. Mrs. Knickerbocker and Mrs. Rudolph were talking just inside the principal's office. The door stood open. Quietly, Cornelia tiptoed closer and peeked inside.

Last year, for the Hallowe'en party, the strict principal had actually surprised everybody by dressing in a black witch's hat and cape. For tonight's party, in honour of Mrs. Rudolph, she was back to her ho-hum principal's clothes. As usual, her ample bosom and backside stretched the fabric of a conservative blue business suit. She wore a maroon necktie, and her hair was piled up in the same grey beehive that could only be called stylin' if you'd been sleeping since the sixties.

"Hey, come on, it's a great look," Irma had once joked, "if you're the new cover girl for *Prison Warden* magazine!"

Mrs. Rudolph, by contrast, had dressed very festively. She wore a bright red jacket with a white fur collar and cuffs in which she reminded Cornelia of a jolly Mrs. Santa Claus. Her greying blonde hair was curled to her chin and looked newly cut, and she was even wearing a bit of make-up.

"Are you nervous, Mrs. Rudolph?" asked Mrs. Knickerbocker.

"I certainly am," replied the plump maths teacher, wringing her hands. "It's strange to think that these are my last hours within these walls."

"Well," said Mrs. Knickerbocker, "look on the bright side. Beyond that gate lies a future full of relaxation."

Mrs. Rudolph shrugged. "Relaxation is something I'm not used to. There's really no telling whether I'll like it or not."

"Just between the two of us," joked Mrs. Knickerbocker, "that's exactly why I've never left my job."

"Maybe you should have told me that before," said Mrs. Rudolph with a smile.

The principal laughed. "Too late," she replied.

Cornelia quickly stepped back as Mrs. Knickerbocker marched out of her office. She headed towards the gymnasium with Mrs. Rudolph right behind her. "Let the party begin!" she called to the crowds of kids flowing into the building.

"Yeaaahhhh!" the kids shouted.

Cornelia moved through the crowd and out the door of the building. She scanned the lawn and finally spotted Irma and Taranee. They were chatting by one of the outside torches. She had just walked up to join the two of them when Hay Lin appeared.

Cornelia turned to greet the air Guardian. Hay Lin looked beautiful. Her two pigtails sported bright pink ribbons at the roots. The ropes of blue-black hair had been lifted high, then tied in bows and fastened in large loops at the back of her head. Her sky-blue coat featured lotus flowers, wide, bell-like sleeves with Asian characters around the cuffs, and a high, straight collar.

Irma and Taranee had dressed up for the party, too. Irma had gathered up her shoulder-length brown hair in a high, cute ponytail and decorated it with a purple flower to match the party dress under her coat. Taranee wore an ocher flower at the top of her black braid. It matched the tawny colour of her ruffled, spaghetti-strap blouse, which she'd worn over ivory–coloured low riders.

"They've turned on the gym lights!" Irma cried excitedly. "Get ready to dance!" She opened her coat and shimmied, making the wide purple skirt of her dress swing from side to side.

"Hang on there, superstar," said Cornelia before Irma could run off. "Before you disappear onto the dance floor, we have something serious to talk about. . . ."

Irma frowned and put her hands on her hips.

I know what she's thinking, Cornelia told herself. I'm a real downer. Well, too bad. Guardian business comes first! She turned to shoot a meaningful look at the air Guardian. "Right, Hay Lin?"

"Unfortunately, it's really simple, guys," Hay Lin began. "Nerissa wasn't defeated like we thought."

Irma's look of annoyance melted into a blank, shocked expression. Her fists dropped limply from her hips to her sides.

Cornelia wasn't surprised at Irma's reaction. This wasn't easy news to hear, not after all they'd suffered together at Nerissa's hands, and certainly not after the ferocious battle they'd waged together in their dreams.

"No," said Taranee. Her brown eyes were now wide with alarm. "That can't be true!"

"But it is true," Hay Lin insisted, stepping closer. "I'm sure of it. Last night I had a strange dream. My grandmother was talking to me . . . and all of a sudden, there was that melody again. I heard it loud and clear. I even heard Nerissa's voice!"

Just then, a group of Sheffield students wandered by, laughing and joking. Hay Lin immediately stopped talking.

Cornelia caught Hay Lin's eye and gestured towards another area of the quad, where they could have more privacy. This was a matter that couldn't be discussed in the open. The entire group moved silently, gliding across the dark lawn like colourfully dressed ghosts.

"She wasn't far from me," Hay Lin continued as they gathered together again in the shadows. "She knew I was listening to her."

"So?" Irma loudly blurted out. "That means we'll never get rid of her!"

Cornelia shot Irma an annoyed look. But she doubted it would have any effect. Quieting the loudmouthed water Guardian with one brief glance was like trying to stop Niagara Falls with a kitchen sponge!

"I still don't want to believe it," said Taranee in a grave tone. "But I guess that somehow Nerissa saved herself from our last battle. And now she must be off somewhere licking her wounds."

"We'll worry about her when she comes back for more," said Cornelia. It was good that the others knew about Nerissa, she thought. But there was a much more important problem they had to deal with. "But right now, our problem is Will."

Taranee's brow wrinkled in confusion.

"What do you mean?"

Cornelia could hear the defensiveness in Taranee's tone. She could see the skepticism in Irma's eyes.

I know what they're thinking, Cornelia warned herself. They know that in the past I've been critical of Will. After all, I was the big Infielder last year, the party planner, the social queen. And I admit I wasn't always comfortable with Will being W.I.T.C.H.'s leader, but that's not what this is about.

Will totally showed us what she's made of, Cornelia thought. She's surprised all of us with her strength, her power, her ability to pull it together and make decisions under pressure. But if the Keeper is not acting like a Keeper, someone else has got to step up.

"Over the last few days, Will hasn't been herself," said Cornelia, her voice rising with her worries. "To me, she seems different . . . edgy . . . *angry*."

"Angry? Even with us?" said Irma, resisting Cornelia's observation. "But we didn't do anything to her. Why don't we just talk to her? Maybe something happened that we don't know about. Maybe she needs our help."

Cornelia fiercely shook her head. "*Or,* maybe Nerissa is behind all of this. For all we know, Nerissa could have attacked her when she was still in the dimension of dreams."

"Attacked her?" Taranee whispered.

Cornelia nodded. "And she might have *won.*"

Irma exhaled a loud, long, disbelieving breath. "Don't you think you're exaggerating? Maybe she's just in a bad mood for some reason or another!"

"That could be," said Cornelia, trying very hard to be patient. "But it could also be a lot more serious."

Taranee folded her arms and met Cornelia's eyes. "Well, what do *you* think we should do?"

Suddenly, Cornelia remembered the terrible exploding fire that Vathek had started at the previous year's Hallowe'en party. Claws of flame had reached out towards Will, threatening to engulf her. But Taranee's instincts had taken over. Even though Taranee hadn't yet been told she was the Guardian in charge of fire, she had summoned her abilities. Without truly realising what she was doing, she had ordered the flames back and saved Will's life when she was in danger.

Now, deep down, a part of Cornelia feared for Will again. "I say we keep an eye on Will," Cornelia advised. "We'll do it without her noticing, but keep your eyes open, all right?"

"OK," Hay Lin said. Taranee slowly nodded. Irma shrugged.

It was a reluctant agreement, Cornelia had to admit, but at least it was an *agreement*.

TEN

From her lair on Mount Thanos, Nerissa waved her dark staff slowly over a volcanic pool. Molten lava rose ominously against an icy cavern wall. The dancing energies pulsed and swirled in a ten-foot-high oval, like a rippling mirror of blue flame.

Inside the swirling blue fire, a series of images began to appear. First came the image of Sheffield Institute. The school was lit up and festively decorated for a nighttime party. Groups of kids crossed the dark lawn and entered the gymnasium. Then came the image of a small group of students – four girls huddled together in an intense conversation.

Nerissa clenched her fists in

fury as she recognised the little Guardians who had fought her so doggedly within the dream realm – and *won*. Her ego was still bruised from losing the battle.

"Irma, Taranee, Cornelia, and Hay Lin," Nerissa muttered through gritted teeth. "The Guardians in charge of water, fire, earth, and air." She could barely contain the disdain in her voice.

Nerissa narrowed her eyes and cocked an ear so that she could hear what the girls were saying to each other.

"I say we keep an eye on Will," the little blond Guardian was advising the others. "We'll do it without her noticing, but keep your eyes open, all right?"

"OK," the others agreed.

Interesting, thought Nerissa with an evil smile, how doubt breeds doubt. "Perhaps it's time I check on the little Keeper now," she murmured.

Nerissa waved her dark staff again. The icy blue lava bubbled and churned. The faces of the four girls disappeared. In their place, Will's image materialised.

The redheaded Keeper wore a sapphire

party dress with a tight bodice, spaghetti straps, and a lace-edged miniskirt. To ward off a chill, she clutched a hooded jacket around her slight body.

Will was hiding behind a stone column in the Sheffield courtyard, listening to her four friends' discussion. None of the other Guardians had noticed that Will was lurking nearby.

Aha, Nerissa thought, it seems I have two things in common with the little Keeper. She likes to eavesdrop, too! Nerissa observed Will's reaction as the young Keeper listened to her friends talk about her.

"So they're going to keep an eye on me, are they?" Will murmured to herself. "I don't know what those four want to find out about me . . . but whatever it is, in one way or another I'll figure it out."

Ah, yes, thought Nerissa. Never underestimate the power of a few nasty rumors. First I get Will to doubt her friends. Then her own paranoid behaviour makes her friends doubt her. Then she doubts her friends even more intensely! It's a perfect, vicious cycle.

"Those voices I heard were right," Will

whispered to herself. "I can't trust anyone . . . not even my so-called friends."

Good, Nerissa thought. My plan is working *perfectly*!

"Will! Finally!"

A scruffy brown-haired boy with stubble on his chin was striding towards Will and waving his hand.

Nerissa looked at the boy. He wore a yellow bucket hat, a worn yellow jacket, and loose red chinos.

Will turned. Her eyes widened at the sight of the lanky young man. "Matt?"

"I wanted to say hi before I started playing," said Matt walking up to her with a huge grin. "Where've you been?"

Will nervously shuffled her feet in her knee-high purple boots. She ran a hand through her shaggy mop of red hair. "I . . . I . . ." She seemed completely tongue-tied.

Matt shoved his hands into his pockets and stepped closer. "Yesterday I was hoping to see you at the shop with your friends. But when I got there, you were gone."

"Oh? Oh, y – yeah?" Will stammered.

Her eyes appeared hypnotised by his

moving lips and the tiny puffs of steam escaping from his mouth in the chilly night air.

"I got the feeling Hay Lin made the whole thing up, just to get a ride!" He laughed. His brown eyes sparkled. "Think she's in love with me?"

Will's face fell. "You . . . you think that?"

"Matt!" called a boy walking towards them. "Matt! Come on, we have to go. They're waiting for us!"

The second boy had spiky blonde hair and a long yellow goatee. Another boy was with him. His straight auburn hair fell well past his shoulders.

"My band's calling," Matt told Will, pointing to the two guys. "Gotta go. Maybe we can see each other during a break. I really don't want to stay up on that stage all night; got it?" He pointed a finger at her and grinned again.

Before Will could respond, the boy with the spiky blonde hair grabbed Matt by the arm and pulled him away from the conversation. "Come on! We're late!" he cried.

"OK! OK!" Matt replied, as his fellow band members continued to pull him towards the gymnasium door.

With a small gesture, Nerissa quickly zoomed in on the image of Matt. She took a closer look at his big, brown, long-lashed eyes; his handsome smile; his puppy-dog look, shaggy brown hair, scruffy chin, and strong jaw.

"He's cute, that Matt," Nerissa concluded, folding her arms.

Another little gesture and Nerissa's magical blue flames focused on Will again. The girl had collapsed in a lump. Her shoulders had slumped, her chin was in her hands, her eyes looked anxious and upset.

"*Hmmm,*" muttered Nerissa, tapping her cheek with a long, pointed nail. "So our little Guardian is in love. . . ."

Nerissa shook her head. In her view, love was for fools – like Cassidy. She sneered as she recalled the former Guardian.

Silly little Cassidy, she thought. I destroyed her so long ago, but she *might* have survived. Love was her downfall. Because of love, she delayed turning me in to the Oracle. She hoped and prayed that I would straighten myself out. All the other Guardians felt the same. They were all trying to be my "friends."

But they were *fools*, Nerissa concluded with

a snap of her fingers. The extra time it took them to bring me to justice allowed me to build up my dark powers. So, by the time the Oracle took the Heart from me and gave it to Cassidy for safekeeping, I was strong enough to destroy her!

Nerissa remembered something the Oracle had liked to say about love. *Love weakens the knees and clouds the mind. But what* power *lies behind this weakness. . . .*

What power? Nerissa's mind echoed what the Oracle had said. *None.* And that was his mistake. Love, friendship . . . they're for the pathetic . . . the weak. There is no power behind those things. Baldy was wrong yet again.

Nerissa peered into the icy flames once more. She stared into Will's anxious eyes and realised something else. . . .

"She's in love but she doesn't know how to tell him! Ha-ha-ha!" she laughed. Yet another reason love is for fools, she thought.

Love always made people suffer. Nerissa considered herself above such foolish feelings.

Fwoosh!

With a wave of her staff, the fiery-looking glass exploded against the icy wall.

The unhappy image of Will was gone. But Nerissa didn't need it any longer. She had seen enough.

"Yes, love always makes people suffer," Nerissa repeated with an evil smile. "And this time, my friend, the pain of love will be completely unbearable!"

Then she laughed and laughed and shouted to the sky with maniacal fury, "This is Nerissa's promise!"

ELEVEN

Tibor stepped onto the wide balcony. Around him, the towers of the vast Temple of Candracar rose in stunning grandeur. Their etched crystal walls displayed sacred designs and dazzling gems from every corner of the universe. Beyond him, the sky stretched along an endless horizon. Clouds as light and cheerful as cotton candy floated by, close enough to touch.

Any human being would have stared in awe at this glorious view. But Tibor could see that Yan Lin was too worried to enjoy it.

She gazed blankly at Candracar's staggering blue infinity. When she heard Tibor approach behind her, she turned to face him.

"Waiting is the hardest part," she confessed. "Knowing that something is about to happen, but not knowing what nor when." She sighed deeply.

Tibor stepped closer to the former Guardian. Like her, he was clothed in a robe white enough to hurt human eyes. His skin, or what one could have seen of it through his long white hair and beard, was creased with wrinkles as deep as time itself.

With his quiet strength Tibor had served the Oracle since the beginning. He served him even now. For the Oracle had sensed Yan Lin's distress and sent Tibor to speak to her.

"You sound disturbed, Yan Lin," Tibor quietly observed.

The old Guardian exhaled in frustration. "I thought that the Elders of Candracar were immune to terrestrial feelings, such as anxiousness or anguish," she told him.

Beneath Tibor's white curtain of a beard, his lips lifted in a smile.

Yan Lin has not been in Candracar very long, he thought. She has much to learn about the ways of the Congregation.

"I once thought so myself," he told her, "but you'll soon see that we're not. I realised that twenty thousand years ago!"

Yan Lin shook her head of long silver hair. "Nerissa," she whispered. Her voice quivered with pain and regret. "I still remember the day I met her. I understood right away that she was a special person."

"She was," said Tibor. "*Before* her desire to possess the Heart corrupted her."

"What I can't understand is how that was possible." Yan Lin's posture stiffened. Her almond-shaped eyes narrowed into dark slits. "Why didn't anyone *stop* it from happening?" She stepped closer to Tibor, her voice rising as the questions continued to bubble up. "Why didn't the Oracle stop Nerissa? Why did he allow her to take Cassidy's life?"

Tibor's old eyes immediately flashed a warning at the former Guardian. "Watch what you're saying, Yan Lin!"

Tibor was worried for the Guardians as much as Yan Lin was. But now he was beginning to worry about Yan Lin herself.

After Cassidy's death, Yan Lin's fellow Guardians Kadma and Halinor had blamed the Oracle for what had happened to Cassidy. They had thought he was at fault because he had done nothing to stop Nerissa. They had raged at him, accusing him of failing to prevent Cassidy's death. And they had been banished from Candracar because of it.

There was nothing the Oracle could do to change a being's will. And it had been Kadma's and Halinor's choice to remain blind to that fact. They had stubbornly refused to understand and transcend.

But Yan Lin was different. She had not blamed the Oracle, because she had seen that there were greater forces at work in the universe. She had been able to *rise above* her mortal understanding while still on earth. For that, and for her brave and steadfast service as a Guardian, she had earned her place in Candracar.

Tibor closed his eyes. *Yan Lin, you have a valued place here,* he told her silently. *Do not allow your fears to cloud your higher vision. Now that you are here, do not let yourself descend into anger and doubt.*

Tibor well knew the consequences that were in store for Yan Lin had she continued in that manner. Luba's fate alone had proved that even an Elder of Candracar had to answer for his or her actions. No one was above reproach.

When the Oracle had decided to entrust W.I.T.C.H. with the powers of the Guardians, Luba had disagreed. She'd thought the young girls were too immature and careless to be given such a responsibility. So she'd sabotaged them.

One day, she'd entered the Aura Hall and cast a spell in order to bind four of the Guardians' five Aurameres together. The Aurameres were the colourful orbs that held the Guardians' powers. Binding them together created an explosion that had rocked the Temple and created an Altermere. On earth, four of the Guardians had temporarily lost their powers.

For her betrayal, Luba had stood trial and been punished. Tibor knew that such a fate was not beyond Yan Lin should she have continued in her outbursts against the Oracle.

Yan Lin turned away from Tibor. She shut her eyes and hung her head. "History is repeating itself, Tibor," she said, "and I can't bear it. Just as we left Cassidy all alone . . . today the other Guardians are not with Will. An error of days past is about to be committed once again!"

Tibor's bushy white eyebrows drew together. He raised a finger, preparing to warn Yan Lin once again. But before he could open his mouth, the old Guardian wheeled away from him to stride back inside.

"And once again," she added, before leaving the balcony, "the Oracle isn't there!"

TWELVE

"Excuse me, kids!" called Mrs. Knickerbocker.

Irma looked up to see the principal waddling onto the gymnasium stage.

Shaking her head, Irma checked her watch. Guess it's that time of night, she griped to herself. Time for ol' prison warden Knickerbocker to throw a cold wet blanket on the inmates' fun.

Bam! Bam! Bam!

The principal tapped the microphone in her hand. The resulting sounds were about as subtle as those of a pile driver.

"May I have your attention for a moment?" she demanded, her voice echoing off the gymnasium walls.

The raucous crowd of partying kids took a long minute to quiet down. They had been getting their groove on with Matt's band. Now the members of Cobalt Blue had paused and were standing behind Mrs. Knickerbocker. Wiping sweat from their brows and sipping water from plastic bottles, the band waited for the signal to begin playing again.

Figures, thought Irma. I *could* have used this interruption about thirty minutes ago, when Martin guilted me into getting down with his nerdy dance moves.

She'd been forced to get jiggy with a boy whose idea of cool was to do the funky chicken in front of the entire student body. So, of course, she'd wanted to die.

Luckily, she had managed to extract herself from the prince of geeks. And she was even beginning to make eye contact with a cute, raven-haired, blue-eyed boy from her homeroom. She had been sure he was about to ask her to dance when Mrs. Knickerbocker pulled the OK, Kids, *Stop* Having Fun act.

In total frustration, Irma turned to Hay Lin, Cornelia, and Taranee. "Looks like my theory is correct," she huffed.

"What theory?" asked Hay Lin.

"Principals just can't stand to see students enjoying themselves," she replied. "I'm surprised Knickerbocker waited *this* long to put the brakes on the party train."

"Testing, testing. Can you hear me?" Mrs. Knickerbocker asked the crowd.

"Yes!" cried the kids packing the gym.

"All right, then," said the principal. "You can get back to going wild in a moment. But the time has come to say a fond farewell to your dear teacher – "

"*Former* teacher, if you don't mind!" Mrs. Rudolph joked, stepping out onto the stage to join the principal.

"Yaaaaaay!" cried the crowd, applauding like mad. The Guardians clapped and cheered, too.

Irma put two fingers in her mouth and whistled loudly for the guest of honour.

I've got to admit, she thought, for a teacher who's actually a creepy creature from another world, Mrs. Rudolph is totally da bomb!

A golden spotlight shone down on the teacher. It illuminated the banner over the stage that read: GOODBYE, MRS. RUDOLPH! WE'LL MISS YOU!

"Settle down, kids," she called when they wouldn't stop cheering. "I won't bore you any longer. I just wanted to thank everyone for the wonderful gifts I've received. This is the most enjoyable farewell I could have imagined, and I'll never forget it, rest assured."

Mrs. Rudolph was about to leave the stage when Mrs. Knickerbocker called out, "No more? Is that your speech?"

Mrs. Rudolph smiled, and her plump cheeks looked like little red apples.

Wow, thought Irma, Cornelia was right. With those rosy cheeks and that scarlet coat with the white fur collar and cuffs, our maths teacher really does look like Mrs. Santa Claus. If she says, "Ho-ho-ho," I'm gonna lose it!

"No speech," the teacher told the principal. "And if I were you, Mrs. Knickerbocker," she added, turning to shake her finger, "I wouldn't make one, either."

Now, *there's* a sensible teacher, thought Irma.

"Rudolph, you're the greatest!" shouted Mr. Collins from the crowd.

Irma laughed at their history teacher's enthusiasm. Wow, she thought, somebody's actually twice as happy as me about the no-speech thing.

"No speech, you say?" said Mrs. Knickerbocker. "And I'd prepared such a lovely one." She held up a piece of paper to the crowd. "Well, all right. . . ."

R-r-r-r-r-r-r-i-i-i-i-i-i-p-p-p-p!

The kids hollered and clapped as the principal neatly tore her speech in two.

Irma was sure that she was cheering the loudest. *Awesome,* she thought. Now Matt's band can start playing again!

"I guess . . ." continued the principal over the applause and laughter. "I'll be using *that* speech for *Mr. Collins's* goodbye party!"

In the audience, Mr. Collins gasped loudly. "You mean you'll still be principal when I retire from this school?"

The kids in the gym laughed.

"What a question!" Mrs. Knickerbocker replied. "You should know by now, Mr. Collins, that I *am* this school! Ha-ha-ha!"

"What a lame comeback," moaned Irma as fewer than half of the kids laughed at this last comment. She shook her head and turned to Cornelia, Hay Lin, and Taranee. "You know, it's kind of creepy to hear the principal kid around."

Taranee shrugged. Cornelia rolled her eyes. And Hay Lin frowned.

Now what's with Hay Lin? Irma wondered. But she didn't have to ask her. The air Guardian lifted her arm and pointed.

"Everybody's having fun except Will," she said.

Irma followed the direction of Hay Lin's finger. Across the room, she saw Will standing in the middle of the crowd of students, dressed in her cute little indigo party dress with its flaring miniskirt and spaghetti straps. Although she'd dressed for the party, however, she was talking to the *last* person anyone with a heartbeat could possibly think was *fun* to talk to.

Edna Everett, a short blonde girl in a pale pink gown, was one of the most boring girls in the entire school, in Irma's opinion. She had an annoying nasal voice and all the wit of a turnip. Case in point: tonight was the most electric night of the school year and what was Exciting Edna doing? *Yawning.*

I just don't get it, Irma told herself when she saw Will hanging with Edna. Why in the world would Will choose inhaling Edna's bad breath over partying with her best friends?

"She's been avoiding us all night," Cornelia pointed out.

Irma's eyes narrowed. It was true, of course. But Irma hadn't actually noticed until then. Or maybe she just hadn't wanted to notice. That would have meant acknowledging that Cornelia had been right all along – a fate worse than going to the dentist as far as Irma was concerned.

And in this case, though Irma hated to admit it, the earth girl actually might have been right. After all, Cornelia had already warned the Guardians that something was wrong with Will.

Of course, she'd also advised them to keep an eye on Will from a distance. But Irma was out of patience. Seeing Will with Yawning Edna was the last straw.

"I've had it with this whole situation," Irma snapped. She knew she was totally losing her usual go-with-the-flow jokester cool, but she didn't care. "I'm going over there to talk to her."

"If you manage to – " Cornelia began to advise her. But she didn't get the chance to finish. The rest of her words were swallowed up by the noise of Matt's band's beginning to jam again.

To the rhythms of the drums and bass guitar, Irma wended her way among jumping, twisting bodies, swinging skirts, and kicking boots. When she got to the place where Will and Edna had been talking, she found they'd already left the spot.

Edna seemed to have disappeared. But Irma spotted Will walking towards the refreshment table. She quickened her steps to catch up.

"What would you like?" the waiter at the drink station asked Will.

"An orange soda, thanks," said Will.

Forcing a big smile, Irma took up a position right next to her friend and fellow Guardian. "An orange soda for me, too, please!" she said, with enough brightness to light up a city block.

"Could you wait here a minute?" The waiter asked the two of them. "I'm out of orange soda. If you want, I can go get more from the back room."

Perfect, thought Irma. This should give me a chance to talk some sense into Will!

She turned to begin the conversation – only

to find Will rudely storming away, looking back with a nasty sneer on her face.

"Go ahead and give mine to her," Will called over her shoulder to the drinks guy. "I'm not thirsty any more."

"Hey!" Irma cried.

She couldn't believe Will had just snubbed her so spitefully, and for absolutely no reason – at least none that Irma could figure out.

"Will! Wait a second!" Irma yelled, following her friend.

But Will just sped up, dashing between the dancers on the crowded gymnasium floor. When Irma lost sight of her, she gave up the chase. Still not quite believing what had just happened, she stopped in the middle of the crowded gym, her hands limp at her sides, her mouth open wide enough to catch stray flies.

Cornelia walked up to her, arms crossed. "Good going, Miss Psychology."

Taranee joined the two of them, her expression angry. "We said we'd be keeping an eye on her from a *distance*!" she huffed.

Irma turned to face her friends. That makes *three* Guardians in nasty moods, she thought. Well, I've had just about enough of this!

"I had second thoughts, OK?" she snapped back at Taranee and Cornelia. "Will's our friend, and I wanted to ask what was wrong without beating around the bush."

In fact, she thought, I'm going to ask her right now after all!

Clenching her fists, Irma rushed off in the direction she'd seen Will go. . . . The only trouble was that the crowd was so thick she wasn't exactly sure where her friend had ended up.

In seconds, Irma's determined strides began to slow. I have only *one* question about Will now, she thought. *Where'd she go?!*

THIRTEEN

"Are you leaving so soon?" called Mrs. Rudolph. "Don't go home yet. The party's just getting started."

Will was surprised to see that the guest of honor had followed her out the side door of the gymnasium. The walkway back there was lit with glowing footlights, but the night was dark.

With the fall chill in the air, Will knew she would soon be cold without a coat on. But at the moment, what with her skin overheated from walking through the mass of packed bodies in the gym and her temper overheated from her encounter with Irma – she wasn't feeling the cold just yet.

She turned to her favourite teacher and smiled. "Oh, no, Mrs.

Rudolph. I'm not leaving. I just wanted to get a bit of fresh air."

Boy, was that an understatement, thought Will. Her so-called friends had been staring at her all night. It was awful how they just kept tracking her every move. Who knew what evil gossip they were sharing and spreading? She'd heard enough before the party – and she was sure those warning voices in her mind had been right. She could no longer trust her friends.

Mrs. Rudolph strolled over to her. She looked a little strange all of a sudden. Her eyes shifted left, then right. "Are you alone?" she asked in a deep, quiet voice. "Or are your friends with you?"

"Alone, thank goodness," said Will, her eyes wide.

What does Mrs. Rudolph know? Will wondered. She looks so uncomfortable. That can't be good.

"I've got to talk to you," the maths teacher whispered. There was an odd urgency to her tone. "There's something you have to know. Let's go into the main hallway."

"Did . . . did something happen?" Will

asked, suddenly worried as they started walking through the shadows and towards the school's front entrance.

"I was waiting for the right moment to tell you, Will," said Mrs. Rudolph. They crossed a dark patio, then pushed through the front doors of the school. "You've been in serious danger, my girl."

"Danger?" murmured Will. "What do you mean?"

"Cornelia and the others are setting a trap for you," said the teacher. "You have to be careful. They're not what they seem."

"What?" cried Will. "What are you talking about?" She was suddenly confused. It was one thing to suspect her friends of gossiping about her or flirting with her boyfriend. It was an entirely different thing if they were actually plotting against her. She had never thought they would be capable of that. How could they? She was supposed to be their leader, their uniter. She was the Keeper of the Heart.

Without me, they're nothing, she raged silently.

A chill ran through Will the moment she had that thought. It sounded just like the kind of thought Nerissa might have had, and it made her uneasy to find herself thinking the same way.

Will wasn't used to seeing the school at night. Although the lights were on, the high windows along the long, locker-lined hallway were dark. Eerie shadows stretched out from deep corners, making the school seem much scarier than it did by day.

"The girls were captured by a dark force," Mrs. Rudolph finally told Will. "The girls surrounding you aren't your real friends. They're impostors!"

Will's blood went cold. "Who told you this? How do you know?" she asked. But Mrs. Rudolph was already turning to go.

"Wait!" cried Will.

"There's no time to explain," said the teacher as she headed out the school's front door. "Those creatures are looking for you, and they'll be here any moment."

"Cr – creatures?" stammered Will in horror. "Hold on! I have to know!"

Slam!

The front door closed. Mrs. Rudolph was gone before Will could ask her for any further explanation of her "creatures" remark.

Fwamp!

A second later, all the lights in the main hallway went out.

"Perfect! A blackout is all I need," cried Will. *Things couldn't get any worse.*

FOURTEEN

"The lights went out!" cried Taranee.

She couldn't believe it.

One moment the gym had been a great big party. Strobe lights flashed across writhing bodies. Walls vibrated with the sound of Cobalt Blue's pounding amps. Teachers and students laughed and talked around refreshment tables, washing down frosted cupcakes with soda and punch.

And the next moment the place had become as dark as a cemetery at midnight.

"We must've blown a fuse," said the janitor, heading for the basement door. "We're using a lot of power tonight."

With the lights out and the band silenced, kids formed small, tight groups. Some sat on the gymnasium's bleachers. Others wandered outside to the quad, gathering around the burning torches for both the light and the heat they offered.

"I'm pretty sure Will isn't in the gym," said Taranee. Irma, Hay Lin, and Cornelia agreed, and the four Guardians headed out of the gym.

"Taranee!" called Mrs. Rudolph.

Taranee looked up to see the retiring maths teacher waving at her from across the lawn.

"Will's looking for you and your friends," said Mrs. Rudolph, walking towards her. "I saw her inside the main school building. Hurry! She said it was important."

Good, thought Taranee. It's about time Will came to her senses.

Irma, Cornelia, and Hay Lin headed for the school's front doors. Taranee stayed behind to talk to Mrs. Rudolph.

"Thanks!" she said. Then she lowered her voice. "And afterward, we can have that *talk*." Taranee put special emphasis on the last word. She wanted to show the teacher that she hadn't forgotten her request for help in opening a portal to Metamoor.

For some reason, however, Mrs. Rudolph didn't seem to pick up on Taranee's meaning. "Oh, really?" she replied with a blank look on her face. Then she smiled. "Well, we can do that another time. Right now, I'll leave you to your dear friend."

"But – "

Taranee wasn't finished talking, but the maths teacher didn't seem to care. She quickly turned and walked away.

Shaking her head in confusion, Taranee jogged across the quad to catch up to the other Guardians. "Something funny is going on here," she warned them.

"You're not kidding," said Irma, thinking Taranee was talking about Will. "In my opinion, she's gone nuts. First she runs away, and then she says she's looking for us. I'd like to know what she's got to say for herself."

Taranee pushed up her large, round glasses. "Will isn't the *only* one acting strange. Mrs. Rudolph called me last night. She wanted us to meet as soon as possible. But now she's acting like she forgot!"

"The party must have burned out a few neurons," said Hay Lin with a shrug as the girls reached the school's front entrance.

Climbing the six stone steps, they passed between two large columns. They opened one of the huge front doors to the school. With the power out, the main hallway looked downright spooky as they stepped inside. Every step they took seemed to create an unending echo down the corridor.

"You can't see a thing in here," Irma complained.

Taranee agreed. She waited for her eyes to adjust. Slowly, images came into focus. Through the windows, the flickering torches in the quad outside sent distorted shadows against the lockers and bulletin boards. The large clock on the north wall had stopped, its second hand frozen in time.

Cornelia peered down the long hallway into the darkness. "I hope Will isn't trying to play hide-and-seek."

Click!

"We have the light. Now all we need are the camera and some action," Irma joked as the power to the school was restored.

Thank goodness! Taranee thought as she rubbed her eyes beneath her round glasses.

Unfortunately, the sudden brightness felt almost blinding. When her eyes adjusted, she began to make out the main hall, the bulletin board, the restarted clock, and . . . *Will!*

"Actually, Cornelia, I'm not in the mood to play games," said the slender redhead.

Taranee gaped at her best friend. She stood in her short, indigo party dress glaring at them with pure hate in her eyes. Taranee had never seen Will like that. Her fists were clenched, her mouth was set in a grim line, and strands of her shaggy red hair hung in her angry eyes.

"And I can assure you," Will continued, "that you won't be having much *fun* in a minute."

Cornelia stepped forward. "I don't get what you're talking about, Will," she said in a gentle voice.

"Do you get *this?*" Will replied. She lifted both hands and narrowed her eyes on Cornelia.

Kz-z-zak!

A searing ray of energy streamed from Will's palms towards the earth Guardian. Cornelia jumped back in fear. The blast just missed her. It bounced off a locker, leaving the metal badly dented and smoking.

Taranee couldn't believe her eyes. Will was using the power of the Heart to attack her best friends! How could she?

"OK!" shouted Irma, throwing up her hands. "That's it! She's *officially* gone nuts!"

"Will! What's got into you!" Taranee cried in fear. She couldn't believe her friend was acting the way she was.

Will frowned and raised her fists. "My sixth sense put me on guard against all of you," she said. "And I just got confirmation. I was **right** to doubt you – the show's over!"

"What are you *talking* about?!" cried Irma.

But Will didn't explain. Instead, she raised her palms again, and another crackling bolt of energy fired from her hands. This time it flew in Irma's direction.

Z-w-a-ck!

"Aaaaaaghhh!" cried Irma. She tried to leap out of the way but wasn't fast enough. The blast sent her flying down the long, wide hallway.

"I don't know who you are or where you come from," Will shouted at them. "I don't even know who sent you. But I want you to bring back my friends!"

Bending down, Will placed her palms on

the tiled floor. As she sent energy into its surface, it began to rumble and shake.

Omigosh, thought Taranee, watching the floor undulate and the tiles fly in all directions, Will's going to destroy the whole place!

All four Guardians were knocked off balance. Suddenly, Will flew at Cornelia, kicking out with her purple-booted foot. "Ooof!" Cornelia cried, doubling over as Will knocked the wind out of her.

Next Will sent a fiery bolt towards Hay Lin. *Whooooooosh!*

She'd aimed too high. The bolt missed Hay Lin's head by inches and hit the edge of a doorway instead, splintering its frame.

Kr-a-ack!

"*Eeek!*" Hay Lin shrieked, shielding her eyes from the flying shards of wood. "Run!"

Together the four Guardians raced down the long hallway. Taranee ran with the others, feeling the blood pounding in her veins. She wanted to use the full force of her power over fire, but she couldn't, without the help of Will and the Heart.

"Without the Heart of Candracar, we can't transform!" Hay Lin cried.

But there must be some way to fight back, thought Taranee. "We still have our powers," she shouted at the other Guardians as they ran. Their elemental abilities would operate at a fraction of their strength without the Heart. But at least that was *something*!

"Powers?" Will exclaimed, overhearing their words as she chased them. "What are you talking about? You're not the real Guardians. You're just a bunch of liars!" Her face was a grimace of hate as she threw out another burst of destructive energy.

Sha-zak!

"Aaagh!" Taranee yelled. The scorching force punched her in the back like a red-hot fist. She stumbled and fell to the floor.

"Taranee!" Hay Lin cried in alarm.

Dazed by the strength of the attack, Taranee was only half aware of Hay Lin trying to help her up.

Irma raced over to help, too. "Will's gone out of her mind," she spat. "We can't let her destroy us."

"Let's defend ourselves!" Cornelia declared, shaking her fist.

"No!" Hay Lin shouted. "We can't do that!"

Z-krak!

Another burst of energy came at the Guardians. It barely missed Irma and Hay Lin as they worked to get Taranee back on her feet.

"Do you have a better idea, or do you want to stay here and get fried?" Cornelia asked them.

"Come on!" yelled Hay Lin, pointing to an open classroom.

Taranee's arms went around her friends' necks. They helped drag her into the classroom. Cornelia followed and slammed the door shut.

As Taranee took deep breaths to get her strength back, the others quickly shoved the classroom furniture up against the door. They stacked a small table on top of a larger one and piled chairs and desks high.

"Listen," Hay Lin told the others, "the dream I had of my grandma was clear. *Against the force of the wind, the oak tree tries to resist, but in the end it snaps in two. . . .*"

Sha-zak! Sha-zak! Sha-zak!

Taranee could hear the bolts of energy striking outside the classroom door. She realised Will was attacking the wood and trying to splinter it. They didn't have much time.

"We can't be the oak," Hay Lin told her fellow Guardians. "But the reed, by bending with the wind, is still able to stand after the hurricane; we have to be that reed!"

Ka-booom!

In one great explosion of energy, Will had shattered the door and sent the classroom furniture flying. Hay Lin, Irma, Cornelia, and Taranee ducked as desks and chairs flew over their heads.

Will marched through the wreckage with the face of a determined monster. The hatred in her eyes was staggering. She was a machine, ready to strike them down.

"Don't respond!" Hay Lin shouted to her fellow Guardians. "Don't respond to violence! Don't resist! Let the blows slip by!"

As Will sent out a devastating streak of energy, Hay Lin closed her eyes. Her hands joined together in a meditative clasp.

Whoooosh!

The destructive power raced straight for her in a white-hot stream of crackling fire. But the air Guardian refused to return the assault or even dodge it.

"Defend yourselves!" Will angrily shouted. "Defend yourselves!"

"No, Will!" Hay Lin responded. Suddenly, the deadly stream of energy exploded into a dazzling white light.

When the light faded, Hay Lin was still standing. She was completely unharmed. The deadly force hadn't harmed her!

"A protective field," murmured Taranee in shock.

Hay Lin had focused her power with a cosmic intensity Taranee had never seen before. She had surrounded all four of them in a shimmering, translucent bubble of protection.

Cornelia and Irma looked as surprised as Taranee. With gaping mouths, they raised their own hands to touch the bubble of energy in front of them. It rippled like water, but they could not push through it.

"We're not here to fight you," Hay Lin told Will.

Schwaaaam!

Will sent another deadly bolt towards the girls. But the protective bubble extinguished it.

Glancing at one another, Cornelia, Irma, and Taranee all knew what they had to do.

Taking a deep breath, Taranee joined the others as they focused their power. The energy flowing through her wasn't nearly as powerful as it had been in the past, when Will used the Heart to help magnify it. But Taranee wasn't the rookie she'd been a year ago. She was no longer afraid to use her own power. She had pinpoint control if she wanted it – and she wanted it *now*!

Taranee's power over fire joined Cornelia's power over earth, Irma's power over water, and Hay Lin's power over air. Their individual energies reinforced the protective field around them.

"I don't know what's got into you, Will," said Hay Lin, trying once more to get through to their friend. "But we *don't* want to do battle with you."

Hay Lin's eyes were still closed, her hands still tightly clasped. Her concentration, like that of the rest of the Guardians, remained fiercely focused on keeping the protective bubble strong.

Will shook her head. "You've been fooling me!" she raged. "I know that now!"

Shwaammm! Shwamm! Shwammm!

One after the other, bolts of energy fired from Will's palms. Taranee braced for the impact against the bubble. She drew strength from the core of her being and focused.

Phhht, phhht, phhht . . .

One after the other, the bolts were absorbed and snuffed out by the defensive powers of the four Guardians.

"We're your friends, Will!" Hay Lin assured her.

Will was rearing back, about to strike again, when Cornelia spoke.

"Someone's fogged your mind, Will. But if you concentrate, you'll be able to sense that we're telling the truth!"

Will hesitated. She settled her gaze on the four Guardians in the bubble. Cornelia had caused her to stop and think. Will looked into the faces of her fellow Guardians one by one – Irma, Taranee, Cornelia, and Hay Lin. Bit by bit, she saw the truth.

They were her friends.

They had always *been* her friends.

And they always *would* be. . . .

Slowly, Will's mask of rage dissolved. As she lowered her arms, her eyes filled with tears.

"No," she rasped, realising the truth. "No . . ."

Before her eyes, Taranee watched Will crumble, her slight body folding towards the floor. "It can't be. It can't be," Will murmured over and over. "What am I doing? What have I done?"

Taranee glanced at the other Guardians, and they all nodded in silent agreement. Relaxing their focus, they let the protective energy bubble dissolve.

But just as Taranee, Cornelia, Hay Lin, and Irma were about to go towards Will, a familiar voice cried out –

"Attack them!"

Taranee looked up to see Mrs. Rudolph standing in the splintered doorway, pointing at her, Irma, Hay Lin, and Cornelia.

I *knew* something was up with her! Taranee thought.

"You idiot!" the teacher cried, glaring at Will. "Don't let yourself be fooled. Destroy them with your power!"

"Mrs. Rudolph?" Cornelia sputtered in disbelief.

"Aaagh!" Hay Lin cried, holding her head. "'Nerissa's Trill'! I'm hearing it again!"

Will turned towards the kindly-looking maths teacher. She raised an accusing finger. "You . . . you lied to me!" she cried, tears in her eyes. "You forced me into fighting against my own friends!"

"Fine, then; have it your way," said the elderly woman, an evil smile twisting her face. Suddenly, she raised her hand to her head, her face contorted in pain. "Ohhhh," she moaned. Then her body went limp, and she slid to the floor.

Taranee's jaw dropped when she saw a ghostly warrior rising out of Mrs. Rudolph's body. The brute's muscles were covered in blue armor. Shaggy blonde dreadlocks hung around a pale, creepy face that looked like a pasty white mask.

"It looks like you girls are pretty tough," said the giant warrior as his ghostly form solidified into a huge, solid mass.

"It's Shagon!" cried Taranee, recognizing Nerissa's evil servant. "He took on Mrs. Rudolph's appearance!"

"Step aside, Guardians. I have to go," said the brute, raising one of his clawed hands.

Slash!

With a sweep of his arm, he sent a powerful beam of force towards Irma and Taranee. It knocked them across the room.

"No-o-o-o!" they cried.

"But we'll meet again soon, to settle the score once and for all," Shagon promised. Once again he lifted his clawed hand, this time pointing it at Cornelia.

Slaaaaaash!

"Aaagh!" cried the blonde Guardian as Shagon's hateful energy sent her towards the ceiling.

Hay Lin immediately lifted her hands. "Here's a nice cushion of air to soften your fall!" she yelled.

Fwooooosh!

A second later, Cornelia was bouncing on an invisible pillow of air. "Ooof!" she exhaled as she landed softly.

Taranee rose to her feet as quickly as she could. Where is that shaggy jerk? she thought. If he wants to fight, I'll show him the meaning of *fired* up!

She scanned the room but saw no sign of him. "The brute's gone," she said, her fists clenched in frustration.

Well, she told herself, at least I agree with him about one thing. We are definitely going to *settle* this score one way or another. And the sooner the better!

FIFTEEN

"Mrs. Rudolph! Do you feel OK?" Will asked anxiously, crouching down to help the elderly woman sit up.

The maths teacher put a hand to her head. "Oh," she moaned. "I feel so dizzy. What . . . what am I doing here?"

The teacher glanced at the wrecked classroom. Behind her large, square glasses, the woman's eyes grew wide.

Irma came over and put an arm around her. "Don't let appearances fool you," she reassured Mrs. Rudolph. "Everything's fine."

"Irma will help you outside," said Cornelia. "A breath of fresh air will do you good."

As Irma ushered the teacher

out of the classroom, Hay Lin felt unable to hold back. "See that?" she cried to the Guardians, shaking her fist. "I was right! Nerissa is still alive!"

Halfway out the door, Irma rolled her eyes. "I think we figured that out, Hay Lin!" she replied, in a tone that said, *Duh!*

Will stood in the middle of the room, her head down, tears of shame filling her eyes. "I can't believe it. . . . I was fighting *against* you."

Cornelia moved towards Will, her long teal taffeta skirt rustling as it brushed against the furniture scattered and overturned all over the classroom. "It's not your fault," she told Will gently. "That monster might have been controlling you, too."

Will violently shook her head. "No, guys!" she replied. "Shagon was speaking through Mrs. Rudolph. And I fell for it!"

Irma walked back into the room to join the others. They were all exchanging glances, as if they were still worried about Will. But Will barely noticed. She was too upset and angry with herself.

"All of the horrible things I've done over the last few days," she continued, "my being so angry at all of you – that wasn't Shagon's work, or Nerissa's. Those were my own feelings. That was me!"

Will was ashamed, embarrassed, and *frightened* about what she'd done. She'd actually allowed a few whispers of doubt to turn her against her best friends!

How could I have let it happen? Will asked herself over and over, sobs racking her slender body. How could I have done it?

"Will, it's OK," Cornelia whispered.

"Don't cry, Will," said Hay Lin.

"It's all over now," Irma declared.

But Will barely heard the comforting words. Dropping her head into her hands, she heard other words, her own recriminating words. . . .

I'm not worthy to carry the Heart, she told herself silently. They shouldn't trust me with it any more!

"Don't be so hard on yourself, Will," said Taranee, putting an arm around her. "You're just really tired."

"Yeah, right," said Will, lifting her head and angrily wiping away a tear. "Tired of having too much responsibility placed on my shoulders. The weight of having to carry the Heart of

Candracar . . . it's too much for one person."

The other Guardians stared at her in confusion and surprise. Will was the Keeper. Their leader. She shouldn't be talking like that, and they all knew it.

"But now I know what I have to do," Will told them.

With that, Will turned and ran full speed out the classroom door.

Everyone stood still for a second, stunned. Only Irma reacted with anger. "Oh, no, you don't!" she yelled. "I'm not letting you get away another time!"

Irma started to chase Will, but the Keeper was too fast for her. Will spun and threw out her arm. "No, Irma!" she cried. "Don't follow me!"

Thump!

Irma had sprung forward but been stopped by a wall of energy. She bounced backwards, landing on the floor. Using the Heart, Will had sealed the Guardians inside the classroom.

"It's an invisible barrier!" Irma cried.

"There's no way out of here!" Hay Lin exclaimed. "She's blocked off the hallway."

As Will ran towards the front doors, she heard Cornelia shouting to the other Guardians. "Let's go through the classroom window!"

Will stopped and focused the Heart's power once more, to extend the force field around the building.

"What could Will have in mind?" Taranee exclaimed to the others.

Time, thought Will. I need time to think.

Will moved down Sheffield's front steps and across the school grounds. "The girls don't understand," she murmured. "They don't understand how horrible I feel because I ended up hating them. . . ."

The night was black and the air chilly. Will realised she was cold without her jacket. She wrapped her slender arms around her body, rubbing her hands up and down along her bare shoulders. But it didn't help.

She shivered all over, and not just from the night air. This entire episode had frightened her to the core. For weeks, she had worried what might come of carrying the Heart. She dreaded the idea that it might be a curse. She feared that what had happened to Nerissa – turning bad and betraying her fellow Guardians – would one day happen to Will herself.

Well, that day has come, she realised in horror.

"I came here to fight," she whispered. "I came here to break up the group . . . while *they* were *worried* about me and trying to *help* me!"

Will shook her head. Her throat was dry, her heart pounding, her stomach in knots. "I can't take this any more!" she cried.

Shivering, she continued across the school lawn, back towards the quad and the entrance to the gym. "What's happening to me?" she murmured, feeling dizzy and confused. "I thought I was strong, and instead I'm breaking apart!"

By then, Will had wandered close to the entrance to the gym. Torchlight flickered upon the stone pathways, and kids were laughing and talking. Friends were calling to each other in the shadowy dark.

"It's all because of these powers and this role I never wanted in the first place," she whispered to herself. The tears were still coming, and Will rubbed her wet cheeks.

"Will?" called a familiar voice. "Hey, you're crying! What happened? Is everything OK?"

Will looked up to see a familiar, brown-haired boy walking towards her from out of the shadows. "Oh, Matt!" She raced across the grass and threw herself against him. "Matt!"

"Hey!" he exclaimed in surprise, his can of orange soda falling to the ground. He put an arm around her. "What's the matter?"

Will clung to him, her hands clutching at his faded yellow jacket. It was good to feel his strength and warmth.

Then she remembered what had happened at Petch earlier in the week, and she cried even harder.

I imagined such terrible things about Matt and Hay Lin when I saw them together, she thought. I assumed they were flirting. I thought they were betraying me. But they were only kidding around. They were totally innocent.

It was *me* who'd let them down, she continued to herself. I'm the one who believed that saleswoman's whispers. Now I know it was all fake. Now I know how terrible a person I am.

Matt held Will quietly until her tears finally slowed. Finally, through quiet sobs, she whispered, "There's something I've got to tell you."

"Well . . ." he whispered, patting her red hair, "what is it?"

"It's about you, me, about everything around us!" she wailed.

Matt guided her to a secluded part of the quad, near an empty bench and a tall tree. The weather was crisp and clear, the stars a blanket of flickering celestial sparkles in the velvet sky. But Will couldn't appreciate the romantic setting. She was too upset.

"I have to apologise to you," Will said, doing her best to control her crying. "I have to explain everything. Ever since we met I've done nothing but act weird."

Matt smiled. "Well, I can't deny that."

"But there's a reason for it all," she insisted.

"Will, you don't have to justify anything," he assured her, turning her to face him. "The moment I met you, I could tell that you were someone special."

Will swallowed and held her breath. *I love you, Matt*, she thought. Please tell me the same thing. *Please!*

"You're unique," he said instead. "You're unpredictable . . . surprising . . . but you're certainly not *weird*."

Tell me that you love me, she thought again. Tell me.

"I'd say the right word is . . ."

Will swallowed, waiting for him to say it.

"Indispensable!" he finished.

With disappointment, Will looked into Matt's big, brown, long-lashed eyes. She bit her lip. "Matt . . ."

"Yes?"

Will knew that what she was about to do was wrong . . . that it would break all the rules. But she'd been so full of doubts that past week, she really needed a friend to lean on.

"I have to tell you a story," she began. "A story that all began with this."

Closing her eyes, Will called silently on the Heart of Candracar. It emerged from within her slight body and appeared like a dazzling pink star in her hand.

"Huh?" Matt cried in surprise when Will showed him the Heart. The crystal's light was so blinding that he had to shield his eyes to look at it.

Will knew she shouldn't be doing what she was doing. She knew that it was a betrayal of the confidence of the other Guardians. It was a betrayal of the Oracle, of the Heart, and of her duty. But she felt *so* lost and desperate. She'd have done almost anything just to hear Matt say that it would all be OK.

It's time now, Will concluded. Time to tell Matt *everything*.

WELL? WHAT ARE YOU WAITING FOR?

IT'S NO GOOD. WILL'S BARRIER HAS SURROUNDED THE ENTIRE BUILDING.

LET'S USE OUR POWERS. WE CAN MANAGE EVEN WITHOUT THE HEART OF CANDRACAR.

FZZZZ

ZZZAN

BACK TO THE DRAWING BOARD . . .

LET'S ALL TRY TOGETHER. ON THE COUNT OF THREE! ARE YOU READY?

ONE . . .

TWO . . .

REALLY NICE JOB, GUYS! BUT NOW WE'D BETTER PUT EVERYTHING BACK IN ORDER BEFORE THIS ALARM ATTRACTS COMPANY.

THE COAST IS CLEAR. THE INVISIBLE WALL'S GONE!

LET'S MOVE. WE CAN'T LET ANYBODY FIND US HERE IN THE MIDDLE OF THIS MESS.

WHAT'S GOING ON?

THE FIRE ALARM'S GONE OFF, MRS. KNICKERBOCKER.

GOOD HEAVENS! WHY IS IT THAT EVERY TIME I THROW A PARTY, MY SCHOOL HAS TO CATCH FIRE?

DON'T... DON'T LOOK AT US, MA'AM! WE DIDN'T HAVE ANYTHING TO DO WITH IT THIS TIME!

WHAT WAS THAT?

I DIDN'T HEAR ANYTHING . . .

I'M STILL TRYING TO TAKE IN EVERYTHING YOU JUST TOLD ME.

NOW THAT YOU KNOW THE TRUTH, ARE YOU SCARED OF ME?

ARE YOU KIDDING, WILL? IT'S . . . IT'S JUST THAT I STILL CAN'T BELIEVE EVERYTHING THAT'S HAPPENED TO YOU.

I MEAN, WE'RE TALKING ABOUT MAGIC . . . PARALLEL DIMENSIONS . . . MONSTERS . . . SOME KIND OF VEIL . . .

. . . AND THEN THERE'S THAT GLOWING THING!

THIS "THING" WAS MY SECRET. BY TALKING ABOUT IT, I'VE BROKEN EVERY RULE.

. . . CAN YOU KEEP THIS SECRET FOR ME?

I HOPE – I HOPE THIS ISN'T A JOKE, WILL, BECAUSE I'D NEVER FORGIVE YOU IF IT WAS . . .

I'VE NEVER BEEN MORE SERIOUS IN MY ENTIRE LIFE. THIS IS NO TRICK, MATT.

CAN I – CAN I HOLD IT?

HERE . . . DON'T BE AFRAID . . .

FALSE ALARM, MA'AM! IT WENT OFF BECAUSE OF A SHORT CIRCUIT. IT'S ALL WORKING NOW.

IT'S NOT IMPORTANT. THE PARTY'S ALREADY OVER.

FIRST THAT STRANGE BLACKOUT, THEN THE FIRE ALARM . . .

. . . AND THEN OUR LEAD SINGER PASSES OUT! I HAD HOPED TO OFFER YOU A MORE RELAXING FAREWELL CEREMONY.

I WAS A BIT OVERWHELMED MYSELF! IT SEEMS I'M NOT USED TO THESE KINDS OF THINGS!

IS MR. OLSEN FEELING BETTER?

OH, YES! HE JUST HAD A LITTLE DIZZY SPELL, THAT'S ALL.

IT'S ALL OK! HE'S FINE . . . AND HE DOESN'T REMEMBER A THING!

HEAR THAT, WILL? YOU SHOULD BE HAPPY.

HAPPY? DO YOU REALISE WHAT I DID?

OK, SO WE DON'T HAVE THE HEART OF CANDRACAR ANYMORE, BUT WE STILL HAVE OUR POWERS. THEY MAY BE WEAKER, BUT WE STILL HAVE THEM. LET'S JUST HOPE THAT WE WON'T NEED TO TRAVEL TO CANDRACAR ANYTIME SOON.